MW00654796

The

Last

Yard Sale

by Marie LeClaire

Soul Attitudes Press
Pinellas Park, Florida

Soul Attitude Press
Pinellas Park, FL

ISBN KINDLE 978-1-946338-23-5
ISBN EPUB 978-1-946338-24-2
ISBN Print 978-1-946338-22-8

Cover Art by SelfPubBookCovers.com/ TerriGostolaPhotography

We must be willing to relinquish the life we've planned, so as to have the life that is waiting for us.

- Joseph Campbell

Chapter 1

It was the end of a long hot Saturday and Marybeth was approaching exhaustion. Twelve yard sales was just too much for one day and she made a mental note not to do it again. Nonetheless, it had ended perfectly, with a carload of merchandise for her store and a little cash left over. Her last stop, as usual, was to pick up things for the Jefferson County Woman's Shelter. Today she came away with a toaster oven and coffee maker along with some children's clothing. Now, tired and hungry, she was making her way home.

The GPS directions had put her on an unfamiliar country road. As she came around a bend, the sign immediately caught her eye. YARD SALE was painted on an old piece of wood and nailed to a tree at the end of a dirt road. It sparkled, iridescent-like, in the afternoon sun. She let out a sigh. As tired as she was, she knew she couldn't resist the prospect of one more bargain, so she turned down the small dirt road, hoping it wouldn't be too far out of her way.

The road twisted and turned through the woods, passing houses generously separated by trees. She'd almost given up, assuming that the seller had closed up for the day. Then she spotted it. A quaint house at the dead end with a long table set up on the lawn. An old woman was seated in a rocking chair under the shade of a maple tree, fanning herself from the unusually warm October afternoon. Marybeth guessed her to be close to eighty. She couldn't imagine what the old woman wanted to sell that would keep her sitting out in the heat all day.

As she pulled up in front, she directed her attention to the items sitting on the table in the afternoon sun. Only four items remained, neatly arranged on a clean wooden table. No mismatched silverware or broken children's toys. No tired paperbacks or old records. Just these four seemingly unrelated things, sitting in the late-day sun.

"Good afternoon," Marybeth greeted the woman as she got out of her car and approached the table.

The woman simply nodded.

"This is an odd selection for the end of the day."

"These are things," the woman began slowly, "I have held onto for far too long. So, they are for sale but choose wisely. The intricacies of each item are greatly understated."

Her curiosity was peaked as she approached the table. Immediately noticing that there were no prices indicated, she wondered how hard a bargain the old woman could drive. As if she heard Marybeth's thoughts, the old woman began to speak.

"Of course, sale is not quite accurate, really. Each item is free, by your way of thinking and yet each has a price of its own."

Before Marybeth could ask for clarity the old woman went on.

"These items are both treasure and trash. They are things I have held tightly to my entire life and I no longer want the burden of them."

She stood in front of the first item. It was a baby doll in near perfect condition. It had an old-fashioned cloth body with a white bonnet surrounding a small porcelain face. There was something odd about it that she couldn't put her finger on, like it was too perfect, considering how old it must be. When she picked it up, the soft body yielded easily to her touch. It felt warm in her hands. Then the heat seemed to travel up her arms, moving quickly, gently enveloping her body. Things became a blur and images began to flash through her mind from a long ago era.

* * *

Suddenly before her was this old woman as a teenager – somehow Marybeth knew it was her – who was left in charge of her much younger sister. The older girl, resentful of the responsibility, was less than attentive to her sibling who had wondered out into the front yard chasing a butterfly. The small girl was so consumed with her new friend that she didn't see the car coming around the corner. Looking up, the teenager realized her sister was gone and with an exasperated sigh, went looking for her. As the teenager rounded the corner of the house, the doll fell at her feet. She looked up to see her sister's lifeless body several yards from where the car had struck her.

* * *

Marybeth came out of the vision slightly off balance. She reached out to the table to steady herself as she looked around trying to reorient. Everything appeared to be back to normal. The old woman was crying silently as she rocked.

"Yes, that's a tough one still," she said quietly. "Do you have a sister?"

It took Marybeth a moment to realize that the old woman had asked her a question.

"Yes," Marybeth stammered. She wasn't sure how

to react. Had the women seen the vision too? Had she known it would happen? What *had* just happened? The woman's nonchalance added another layer of bizarre to the experience. Marybeth forced herself to focus on the question. She thought about her sister and her heart sank a little. She hadn't spoken much to her sister since the divorce. Regina had been harsh with her, accusing her of shutting her out emotionally. Marybeth couldn't completely blame her for that. She had covered up and minimized the problems in her marriage for years. When she had finally had enough, everyone seemed shocked, including her husband. Nonetheless, her sister's criticism had left a strain on their relationship, mostly because she knew Regina was right.

Marybeth gingerly put the doll back down on the table and moved to the next item, a beautiful porcelain music box with a bride and groom dancing happily-ever-after on top.

"Ah, yes," crooned the old woman, "Fifty-one years together we had when he died, not all good years I'll say, but not so bad mostly. He didn't hit me and he didn't drink his paycheck. That was pretty much the measuring stick back then of a good man so I suppose by those standards, he measured up okay. I don't know that I ever really loved him though. Not in *that* way, the way we are always promised as young girls. It was more of a practical endeavor."

As Marybeth picked it up, the music box began playing Louis Armstrong's "A Kiss To Build A Dream On"...the song she and her ex-husband had danced to at their wedding.

* * *

Mary Beth let out a quiet gasp as the vision unfolded of her own wedding when she and Eric had twirled around the floor the floor in the traditional first dance. She was already having second thoughts even before the music ended. Barely able to admit it now, she had felt misgivings for some time before the wedding. Desperate to be married and start a family, she had convinced herself to push forward. Her plan was to be well established with husband, job and home before her first baby. But she was growing aware of her biological clock and offers for happily ever after hadn't been exactly flooding in. Eric seemed as good a partner as any. So she continued to discount the red flags hoping that household responsibilities would make things better. Thus began what would become her marriage mantra "It will get better when. . ."

* * *

The music box still played in her hand as she became conscious of the yard again. Again, she looked around wondering if anyone was watching. She and the old woman were the only ones in sight.

"Are you married?" the old woman asked.

"Divorced," Marybeth stammered. Recalling the old woman's description of her own marriage she added, "He didn't hit me and he didn't drink his paycheck."

"I understand," the woman said with a nod.

Curiosity took over her common sense as she cautiously moved to the next item. It was an old sepia photograph of a young man with five children.

"I was the middle one," the old woman offered, "just eight years old when my mother died in childbirth. It's hard to believe it now, but I took care of the young ones while the older ones went to work. I wasted too many years being angry about that."

Marybeth reached out for the photo.

* * *

The world went into a foggy spin and when things cleared Marybeth found herself in a small chapel with a half open casket at the front. An eight-year-old girl was in a tearful rage screaming "I hate you! I hate you!" at the body of a young woman lying in repose. An older man rose from his seat and gently carried the young girl out of the room.

* * *

Back on the lawn again, the memory of her parents' divorce forced itself into her mind. She had felt abandoned and scared at the time. Over the years those emotions had changed to anger. Was she starting to see a pattern here of her own life told through the old woman's stories?

She steadied herself as she remembered the pain and anger from that time. The woman's words shook her out of her reflection.

"Family's family," she said. "In the toughest times, it's always family you want, no matter what."

The truth of this statement shot directly into her heart. In her toughest times, she had shut everyone out when what she really needed was family.

The last item for sale was an old book with a white leather cover accompanied by a white shawl. It smacked of religion, a topic she avoided at all cost. She and God had parted company when the last of her fertility treatments failed. Nonetheless, she picked it up and fanned the pages. She glimpsed what appeared to be a selection of songs and poems just before a vision altered her awareness once again.

* * *

She was transported to a beautiful church

where people were blissfully raising their voices in song. Some swayed or clapped their hands. As the hymn came to a close, Marybeth looked around for the preacher. Was this lecture going to be a guilt trip about divorce? She still felt bad about it sometimes. Had she really done all she could to save her marriage? Or maybe to finally explain the punishment of life without children? To her surprise, she saw a young dark haired woman standing in the sanctuary draped in a green veil with gold trim. when the young woman looked directly at her and began to speak.

"There is only love, Marybeth. God is only love. Divine, eternal and pure. God is not about forgiveness or punishment because there is no need for these things when there is only love. When you allow yourself to experience this love again, you will heal your heart."

Shocked to be addressed directly, her instinct was to push back, argue the point, but something stopped her. The woman's words reached deep into her soul, directly contradicting the harsh religion of her youth and stirring up an old pot of emotions which Marybeth immediately shut down.

* * *

Again, she was back on the lawn, trying to get her bearings, looking at four items that didn't seem to be much of a bargain at all. Were these things haunted or cursed? Was she losing her mind? Before her brain could make a logical decision, the old woman began to speak.

"I should have let these things go a long time ago. Maybe there are things you should let go of."

"I don't know what you're talking about," she shot back more abruptly than she intended.

The woman simply nodded and rocked.

She turned back to the table. "I don't think I want them," she said without looking back.

"There's no charge. You might as well take them," came the woman's reply.

Not wanting to pass up *free*, she rationalized, "Well, I collect things for the Jefferson County Women's Shelter. I suppose they can use them."

"As you like," was the woman's reply.

"Can I take them all?"

"You surely can," replied the old woman. "I'm done with them."

Marybeth spotted a box under the table and, after cautiously wrapping each one in newspaper, loaded the box into the back of her jeep. She turned to say thank you to the old woman but she was gone. The rocking chair sat unmoving under the tree.

Marybeth looked around quickly. Where was she? And where was everyone else? Neighbors? Cars driving by? The hair on the back of her neck started to rise. As quickly as she could, without actually running, she jumped into the driver's seat and headed back the way she had come.

Chapter 2

On the drive home, Marybeth played over in her head the strange events at the last yard sale and wondered if she was going crazy. She fought the urge to pull over and check the back of the car for the four new items. Did this whole thing really just happen? Was this all some strange hallucination? She hadn't eaten all day except for a few cookies. Would she get home to find no last minute items in her car? She was quietly hoping that the items wouldn't be there. Better to be crazy than have magical things in her car, she reasoned.

By the time she pulled into her driveway and opened the garage door, she was convinced it was all some kind of daydream. But when she opened the hatch, the box of strange items was tucked neatly into the corner. Suddenly, she was angry at herself.

"Why did I agree to take her junk!? What was I thinking?"

Then she turned her anger at the old woman.

"And who the hell was she?" she asked out loud.

Avoiding the box, she began to unload the back of the jeep into a garage that passed as a workshop. Shelves lined the three walls. Two large tables in the middle provided a multipurpose work surface currently holding works in progress. The rhythm and routine of the task eased her nerves a bit and she started wondering about the other items in her car. What stories could they tell? She crinkled her nose at the musty odor of the old army footlocker as she dragged it out of the car and placed it in the garage.

"I bet you have some good ones." She placed it on the floor under the lowest shelf.

"And what about you?" she asked as she dusted off a mantle clock sitting just above it.

"I can imagine the family drama you've seen play out."

As she touched each item though, no magic, no visions. Once again, she wondered if that last stop had been real.

Yard saleing, started out of necessity, had quickly turned into a hobby and then a small business.

"You need to have your own yard sale," a friend joked when her garage started busting at the seams.

Instead, she had bought a table at a local flea market where she quickly sold out her inventory. After a few months of success, she broke down and began to look for a storefront. It just so happened that a little shop opened up in downtown Pomroy, right at the one traffic light that marked the center of town. She opened her doors two months later with One Woman's Junque – An Antique Boutique.

The workshop had become a refuge from life's turmoil. In the last two years she had ended her marriage, quit her job as a kindergarten teacher, sold her house as a condition of the divorce, and had a falling out with her sister, Regina, who had been her best friend. The news sent Regina, into a rage – not at Eric but at Marybeth.

"What?" Regina asked incredulously when Marybeth told her about the divorce. "How can that be? I don't understand."

"It's been a long time coming," she had replied. "I haven't said anything because I didn't want you to think badly about Eric, you know, if things worked themselves out."

"Really? Because you don't think I have the ability to let go of things as long as you're happy? And to support you and help you work things out? Isn't that what we've always done for each other?" Regina had shot back.

She was surprised by Regina's anger. "No, not at all. It's not like that. I just didn't want you to get in the middle of my mess. I was in pain from all directions and I couldn't even talk about it."

"I knew you shut me out about the baby. I guess I was naive to think you would share other things. What else haven't you told me?" Regina shouted on the way out the door.

The rift between them felt like the Grand Canyon. It was one more thing Marybeth felt guilty about now, but at the time she blamed her sister. They had always shared everything since childhood. But Marybeth felt ashamed by the state of her marriage and her failure to conceive a baby. She couldn't bear to talk about it, even with Regina. When the truth came out, Regina was deeply hurt. The result was a cool distance that seemed to keep growing.

The situation with Regina fueled her anger at Eric. She didn't blame him, really. Okay, maybe she did. Consciously or not, he had mounted a campaign that crushed her spirit. Consciously or not, she had let him. Ever hopeful, she had expected that her joy would eventually rub off on him. Quite the contrary. His constant negative approach to life grew heavy over the years until she couldn't carry it any longer. Add to that six years of unsuccessful fertility treatments and it finally took its toll. In the end, she was just as negative and depressed as he was. Looking back now, she wondered how she survived.

She walked around the garage now appreciating the transformations that occurred here. As she ran her hands over the top of the kitchen table she had just refinished, she remembered the bumps and dents that covered it when she picked it up for $30. The new finish brought out the beauty in the wood and it felt silky smooth to the touch. She was always learning new skills to recreate or restore old things. In the corner was the beautiful Captain's chair she picked up last month. The only thing it had needed was a new cane seat and a little cleaning. Her fingers were raw by the time it was done, but the payoff was a truly beautiful piece of furniture. Over the last two years she had taught herself tole painting, crocheting, macramé, furniture refinishing and stained glass work. She also found she had a creative knack for reinventing items for different purposes. Old picture frames transformed into table tops or fancy mirrors and almost anything could become wall art these days. Last week she spray painted a couple of hub caps, wired them together and hung them in the shop. They sold instantly.

Surveying the garage one more time, she turned her gaze to the driveway. The jeep stood with its hatch up, defiantly announcing the sole remaining item still tucked in .the corner. There was no avoiding it now.

Leaving it till morning would result in a torturous night's sleep worrying about it. She looked up and down the street to make sure no nosy neighbors were watching. Cautiously approaching it, she tapped it then backed off a few times to be sure nothing weird would happen. When she was convinced it was safe, she brought it in and placed it on the other side of garage, away from the rest of the occupants.

"What am I worried about?" she said out loud, "they'll talk to each other?"

Looking at the box, she worried again about her sanity. Shaking her head in disgust, she headed into the house for dinner.

Chapter 3

The silence of the kitchen gave way to a rumble in her stomach. She opened the cupboard in search of dinner. The kitchen's menu options stared at her from the shelf.

"Cheesy potato soup or beef stew. Tough call."

It was sad to see the current state of her kitchen. When they first began fertility treatments, she embraced cooking with a new enthusiasm, educating herself on healthy eating and ways to support her body during pregnancy. She even learned how to make healthy baby food, but when the last attempt at pregnancy failed, she lost all interest in cooking. Now, shopping was a hassle and eating was a chore. Mealtime had become a combination of foraging and creativity. Dinner tonight would be potato soup and toast.

As she ate, she replayed over and over, her last encounter of the day. Who was the old woman in the yard? Had anyone else stopped at the sale that day? Had other people gone home with strange magical items? The words of the seller stuck in her mind, *Maybe there are things you should let go of*. What did she mean? She thought about the baby doll and her sister, Regina. They had grown up one town over from Pomroy, in Westfield. Its claim to fame was the local community college offering two and four year degrees in basic concentrations, and a long forgotten Civil War battlefield that drew in a few die-hard Civil War enthusiasts each year. It was the perfect place to raise children. The large town common was the site of many holiday picnics and celebrations. The 4th of July parade was not complete until the Pet Regiment, dressed in full red, white and blue regalia made its appearance. They tried to dress up Lulu the cat one year. She smiled at the memory, then felt a familiar sadness. No matter how sweet the memories, they all seemed to bring her back to the day her parents announced the divorce. Marybeth hadn't taken it well.

"What? What are you talking about!?" Marybeth demanded. "You can't do this!"

But as calmly as if they were telling the kids it's time for bed, mom and dad explained the changes that were taking place. Dad bought a house nearby, within walking distance, so as not to disrupt their lives much.

Really? she thought now. *Did they really think this would not disrupt their lives much!?*

Regina took the news much better. She helped Marybeth see the up side of divorce, like having a new room to decorate and stuff to buy for the new house. Dad allowed them to be involved in picking out the dishes and curtains and things. It was fun for the moment, but Marybeth was not like Regina and never really accepted the split. The new living arrangement just complicated things for her. Two birthday parties. Two Thanksgiving dinners. Two wardrobes. Two computers. Some kids might have thought it was great, but for Marybeth it was a constant reminder that her family was broken.

It seemed like Regina was the only one she could count on and they were thick as thieves. Occasionally they would walk just on the edge of serious trouble, like the time they were twelve and fourteen and decided to catch the bus to the new shopping mall (without permission of course). They had never ridden the bus and weren't really sure how it worked, but when the bus stopped at the mall, off they hopped.

The mall was huge, much bigger than anything they had seen before. They were wandering around, pie-eyed when they were approached by a couple of older boys who were flirty and seemed very sophisticated.

"Hey, how 'bout if we hang around with you?" the tall one asked.

"Sure," Regina giggled before Marybeth could raise any objection.

The boys walked with them as they went from store to store. It wasn't until a security officer cornered the four of them, that they found out what the boys were really up to. The boys had been shoplifting from each store they entered! $85 worth! She and Regina pleaded complete ignorance, and apparently were convincing. The officer let them call their parents to come pick them up. They called Dad, figuring he was the least likely to freak out. When dad said, "You're on your mother's time. You have to call her." Marybeth lost it, screaming and ranting in the security office. It was Regina who calmed her down, then called their mother. It was a painful moment of realization for her that her family really wasn't getting back together.

Over the years, her pain turned into anger and resentment, and even deeper than that - doubt. Doubt that her world was stable, doubt that the people in her life would be there when she needed them, and doubt that relationships ever worked. This last doubt had recently been reinforced by her own failed marriage. She immediately swerved away from that topic and directed her frustration at the old woman.

"Maybe there are things you should let go of," she repeated mockingly. "What did she mean by that? As if I can just put stuff out at a yard sale and say good-bye to them like she did."

She found herself feeling a little jealous of the old woman, then anger again.

"She got rid of stuff alright, straight to me!"

Why had the old woman given these things to her for free? "Free" didn't sound so good at this moment. She wished she'd asked more questions at the time. But how could she have? She was dazed and confused by the information invading her brain. She decided that tomorrow she would go back to the old woman's house and find out more about these mysterious items and the visions that went with them.

Chapter 4

Marybeth woke up early Sunday morning to the smell of brewing coffee, courtesy of the programming feature on the Cuisinart. She enjoyed Sunday mornings sitting at the kitchen table watching the birds through the window. Her house was small but comfortable for a single woman. It could even be comfortable for a couple, if that opportunity ever looked interesting again. After the demise of her marriage and the financial devastation of the divorce, she didn't think she'd ever consider it, but who knew.

Thoughts of The Box, as she was now referring to it, kept her tossing and turning most of the night, and continued to plague her in the early hours of the morning. Trying to distract herself, she had eaten breakfast and showered by 7:30 a.m. Now she wandered around the house wondering how early she could call on the old woman. A list of questions was developing in her head. Who was the old woman? Why did she have these visions? What was she supposed to do with the items in the The Box? After pacing the kitchen three more times, she decided to go find the house. Maybe the old woman would be outside working in the front yard before the heat of the day or enjoying the quiet morning on the porch. As she backed out of the driveway, she noticed her hands trembling a bit. Too much coffee, she thought, not wanting it to be nerves.

She headed back the way she came the evening before, retracing her trail as best she could remember. It was early on Sunday morning and the country roads still held onto the quiet of dawn. A few birds dipped past her car but no other activity disturbed the peace. She turned down the road she was sure had led to the yard sale. It turned to dirt shortly after leaving the main road and had grass growing down the middle as she went further along. The road dead-ended just as it had yesterday but the last house was not the same. Again, she noticed the trembling in her hands, now joined by a quickened heartbeat. What was going on? Thinking she was confused, she decided this was the wrong street and turned around. She spent the next two hours driving down every country road she could find, trying desperately to retrace her steps from yesterday. Finally, defeated and disoriented, she headed home.

She threw the box back in the corner, giving it a kick for good measure before sitting down on the footlocker she had purchased the day before.

"What is happening to me?"

This kind of thing wasn't supposed to happen, at least not to her. Some people seemed to have knowledge to other realms or claimed they did. She believed that there was something beyond this existence, but conventional religion seemed a bit too heavy on the guilt and shame for her taste. The new age stuff had held some promise for her, until she saw the woman who claimed to channel deceased pets from their new home on Saturn or the Angel Whisperer who could talk to the dead and ask spirits to manipulate life's circumstances. Even if she bought into any of these ideas, none of them helped her understand what was happening. She needed to make sense of things quickly, fearing she would go crazy if she didn't. She leaned over and looked into The Box.

On top, looking up at her, was the baby doll. She remembered vividly the images associated with this item from the day before. Hesitant to pick it up again, she convinced herself she was being silly and should attend to it like any other yard sale item. Taking a deep breath, she reached for the doll. Nothing happened. She picked it up, looked at it, turned it over, then closed her eyes, anticipating some strange experience. Nothing happened. Today it seemed to be just a doll. Again, she questioned her memory and her sanity. She was reluctant to move the doll into the resale pile just yet. What if someone else picked it up and had some weird kind of episode? It might not be *safe* to put in the store. As she contemplated what to do with it, the phone rang. She ran into the house to catch it, taking the doll with her.

She looked at the caller ID and was surprised to see Regina's name on the display. These days, Regina rarely called her unless something was wrong. A knot tightened in her stomach. Had she somehow known of Marybeth's musings last night? That would be hard to believe, but a lot of things were suddenly hard to believe. She gingerly picked up the phone as if it might electrocute her. "Hello?" she said.

"Hello, Marybeth, it's me, Reggie."

They hadn't been *not* talking, but they had carefully avoided each other since their argument two years ago. Marybeth felt badly about it. She understood why her sister felt hurt and could admit to herself at least that she had, in fact, cut her sister off emotionally. She had cut everyone off, choosing instead to suck in all the pain until it threatened to destroy her. In hindsight, not the best plan she ever had. Now, she couldn't see how to get across the great divide that had developed since then.

"Can I invite myself over for lunch?" Regina tentatively began.

"Ah, sure Reggie." She said, not having a good reason to say no.

"I'll be there in a few." Regina hung up before either one could take the conversation any further. Marybeth looked into the dead phone and then down at the doll in her hand. Her pulse quickened a bit, wondering if this was the moment of truth for them. She should have cleared the air two years ago but there was so much chaos back then. And, after all, Regina hadn't tried to reach out to her, either. Emotional exhaustion had stopped her then. Now it was flat out avoidance.

Regina only lived two miles away and she really would arrive in just a few minutes. Marybeth started rushing around the house, straightening up the living room and putting clutter out of sight. Looking at the doll still in her hand, she stuck it quickly up on the mantle and headed back to the kitchen looking for something to eat.

She knew the cupboards were mostly bare. Peanut butter and jelly, a few cans of soup, and the beef stew she passed over the night before. Peanut butter was out. Her sister was severely allergic. Jelly sandwiches and soup? Not very appealing. She defaulted to their old standby – coffee. It was a love they had shared since college when they would sit for hours drinking and talking. Would this be one of those times?

As promised, in just a few minutes, there was a knock at the kitchen door.

"Hello?" Regina called into the house.

Marybeth welcomed her with a polite hug and was just about to apologize for the lack of lunch when she noticed Regina was carrying a bag.

"I whipped up a couple of egg salad sandwiches and chips," she said almost apologetically.

"Great. Thanks. I haven't been grocery shopping in a while."

"Yes, I remembered you hate that since. . . so, anyway, I came prepared."

"How are things going?" they both asked at the same time.

"Oh sorry."

"No you go first." They both continued awkwardly talking over each other.

"How about some coffee?" Marybeth finally got in.

"That would be great. Thanks."

She poured them both a cup of coffee and sat down at the kitchen table. The lunch bag sat untouched. They sipped their coffee in an awkward silence until finally Regina started off.

"How have you been?"

"It's been a mixed bag, you know, lots of changes, some easy, some not so much. How 'bout you?" They both silently agreed on small talk.

Regina continued the small talk cautiously. "Same for me. I moved in with Tony. That's been good. We'd love to have you over for dinner one of these days." Regina grimaced as she realized how lame the invitation sounded.

God, Marybeth thought, how much harder can this get! She stared down at her coffee. In her heart she knew the first apology was hers to make.

"Look, Reggie, we both know things have been

hard for of us for a while and I'm sorry. I know I carry a lot of responsibility for that." The words rolled off her lips as if she had rehearsed them many times, which she had. "You were right. I shut down and shut everyone out, including you. I kept things to myself, maybe hoping to avoid my own pain. It was a bad idea." She looked up to gauge her sister's response.

It was Regina's turn to look down at her coffee. "I couldn't understand why you didn't talk to me about things. I was hurt and I said a lot of things I shouldn't have. I'm sorry for that. Now that I have my own relationship, things look different."

"I know. At the time I felt like you wouldn't understand. Now I get it that I didn't give you a chance to understand or not."

"What did you think I wouldn't understand?" Regina had a pleading tone in her voice.

"First of all, the whole pregnancy thing."

"Like what?"

Marybeth paused looking for the words she wanted and bracing herself for her own pain. She folded her hands together to steady herself. "The in-vitro thing. Most people don't understand the indignities of it all. It sounds nice, but it's not. The procedures are embarrassing and time consuming, and they have a low success rate. You don't want to tell people because you don't want to deal with all the questions about how it's going and, of course, the inevitable, "Are you pregnant yet?" She looked up to see Regina grimacing.

"I was one of those people, huh?" she asked.

Marybeth shrugged and went on. "You have no idea how painful it is. It sucks the joy out of you. At least I can say that's how it was for me. I'm sure it's different for some couples. Maybe if I had gotten pregnant it would have all seemed worth it. But I didn't. And I just couldn't talk about it." She looked down at her hands and shook her head.

"I've had just as long as you have to think about things. I can see how my enthusiasm might have made things worse. I just wanted to be your best cheerleader, like always."

"I know you did, but you didn't let me feel how I felt, which was defeated, embarrassed, ashamed."

"Ashamed!" Regina interrupted with surprise. "But why?"

"I felt like God didn't think I was good enough to be a mother or that somehow this was punishment for something." Marybeth sat back distancing herself from her sister.

"But you know that's ridiculous, right?" Regina jumped in.

"Yes, and no. It's way more complicated that you think and I felt like I couldn't have these conversations with you because, like just now, you won't let me have my feelings."

"But..." Regina stared to defend herself, then stopped. "Okay, I get it. I didn't allow you any space to have the negative feelings about things. Why didn't you say something at the time?"

"I did. You didn't hear me."

"I'm so sorry," Regina was lost for what else to say.

"Add to that the financial stress brought on by the medical bills and the fact that somewhere along the way, Eric started spending money on crazy stuff."

"What do you mean? I had no idea!"

"Yeah." Marybeth paused in reflection. "One day he decided we both needed bicycles and bought them without even having a conversation with me. $2,500 worth. We never even used them."

"Oh no." Regina said sympathetically.

"And then there was the contractor he paid $500, cash of course, to seal the driveway, who was never seen again. And the $400 watch he bought me for a birthday present even though we couldn't pay the mortgage."

"Oh my God."

"I couldn't keep up with what he was doing. I felt like I had to micromanage him. Money became a constant argument and in the end we were under crushing financial stress too."

"I wish you had told me," Regina said quietly.

They sat in silence, each beginning to understand the other's pain.

Marybeth had been keeping the coffee cups full and they were waiting on the second pot to finish dripping when Regina finally said "How 'bout we eat these sandwiches?"

"I've got a better idea." She opened a cupboard, reached up to the top shelf and pulled out a large blue tin of butter cookies. She held it up for approval.

A smile lit up Regina's face as she pointed at the tin. "That's what I'm talkin' about".

They both laughed. "Let's go sit in the living room. It's more comfortable than these kitchen chairs." Marybeth grabbed the pot of coffee and led the way. Regina grabbed their cups and followed after her.

As they rounded the corner, Regina looked around the room, taking in the new home her sister had created in her absence. She noticed all the little things she knew her sister loved like the geranium drooping over the mantel. Then her eyes landed on the doll.

"What's this?" Her smile faded a bit? She placed

the coffee cups on the table and asked with in a shaky voice "Where did you get this?"

Marybeth, puzzled by the reaction and not wanting to complicate things, simply replied "at a yard sale".

"I had one like it when we were little," Regina said.

"Really? I don't remember that." Marybeth turned away, putting cookies and coffee pot on the table.

"I didn't play with it much." Her voice was soft as she gathered the memory from somewhere in the back of her brain. Then she gently took the small toy off the shelf.

Marybeth looked up to see her holding the doll and before she could say anything, her sister froze, still holding the doll in the air.

Chapter 5

As she picked up the doll, Regina was immediately transported back in time to when she had held her own doll. It was the night their parents told them about the divorce.

* * *

She saw her younger self sitting on the couch, holding the doll tight to her belly. Her dad had given it to her a few weeks earlier, for her sixth birthday. She adored her dad and always tried hard to win his approval, but she knew Marybeth was his favorite. Marybeth always got the new stuff and she always got the hand-me-downs. It was only on special occasions like birthdays that she got something entirely her own. She knew her dad had picked this doll out for her. She had seen him sneak in the day before with the bag from The Antique Doll House, her very favorite store.

Regina listened to her parents talk about the changes ahead. She felt as if all the blood were draining out of her body and soon she would disappear entirely. It wasn't long before she couldn't hear them at all, like watching a movie without the sound. She was sure if she had just done something different, her dad would have loved her more and her parents would have stayed together. Guilt and panic crept in slowly.

When the girls were sent off to bed, Regina ran to her room and closed the door before anyone could see her distress. She grabbed the doll and in a fit of six-year-old rage, she threw it into the back of her closet. She flung herself onto the closet floor and began weeping the full-body sobs of the inconsolable. She remained this way, swallowed up by betrayal, fear and guilt for what seemed like hours. Then suddenly a warm light began to illuminate the closet, gradually growing brighter. It centered around a beautiful woman draped in sparkling green silk, more beautiful than anything she had ever seen. The woman spoke to her in the kindest voice Regina had ever heard. She felt as if an angel had reached into her body and gently washed away all her pain. "We are always with you", the woman said, "watching over you and protecting you. You are a perfect child of God and you have done nothing wrong. You must help your sister during this time with your gift of laughter. This is your job in this life, little one, to help your sister and others to laugh. As long as you are both laughing together, life will be good."

* * *

Regina stumbled as she came out of her vision. She reached out to steady herself with the mantle. Then suddenly burst into tears clutching the baby doll to her belly. She turned to Marybeth and said through her tears, "Oh my God, I remember." Marybeth rushed to her side and lead her to a chair. Regina took a few deep breaths to regain her composure then turned to her sister.

"What the hell just happened?"

"I'm not sure but I can guess." She wrung her hands, hesitating to go on. "Did you just, uh, see something weird?" she said cautiously.

"Yes, I did. Are you going to tell me about it?" Regina nearly demanded an explanation.

"Yeah, well," Marybeth eased in, "I got the doll at a yard sale yesterday, a very strange yard sale. I started having these, well, sort of, visions. Is that like what happened to you just now?"

"Why didn't you tell me!? Warn me? Is this more shit you're not telling me?" Regina felt the anger rising.

"No. No. No. It's not like that"

"Then what is it like?"

"I'll tell you everything, I swear. First, are you okay? Tell me what happened." If Regina had had a vision too, then maybe she wasn't going crazy. And if she was, then at least Regina was going right along with her.

Taking another deep breath, Regina began, "Do you remember the night mom and dad told us about the divorce?"

"Like it was yesterday."

Well, I've never told anyone this before, but...." Regina slowly and quietly told her sister about the vision she just had and about the vision she had experienced when she was six, on the day the divorce news was delivered.

"I don't remember that doll at all."

"I didn't play with it at all after that night. It stayed in the back of my closet at Mom's. As far as I know, it's still there. I totally forgot about it until just now. What ever happened to mom and dad? I thought they were perfect for each other."

"Yeah, me too."

Their parents were both professors at Jefferson County Community College in Westfield. Her mother taught English and her father taught math. As a child,

she had thought it was the perfect match. Now she
realized that they were two people who saw the world
completely differently. Mom saw the world in colors
and dad saw the world in numbers. Mom saw into the
essence of things. Dad needed proof of everything. The
old adage "opposites attract" might be true but
Marybeth wondered if opposites ever really went the
distance.

As they started to share their different experiences
of that day, they realized, to their surprise, they had
never really talked about it. At ages eight and six, what
was there to say exactly. Then life just went from one
moment to the next, changing and changing again,
without much conversation or awareness. Now, as
adults, they had an entirely different context for it.
Regina realized that the feelings she had about
Marybeth's divorce were the same feelings she
experienced back then, of being emotionally shut out or
that somehow it was her fault or maybe she could have
helped fix things.

"When you told me about your divorce, I felt the
same kick in the gut I felt back then. I felt like I
couldn't get mad at mom and dad so maybe I took the
opportunity to get mad at you instead. Funny how
things from so long ago can sneak into the present."

"Yeah. I've realized recently one of the reasons I
stayed with Eric for as long as I did was to show mom
and dad you can work things out if you just try hard
enough. You can see how well that worked. I have a
whole new appreciation for what they went through. At
least their divorce was peaceful, as much as I
remember, anyway."

"I don't remember them fighting a lot either, before
or after the divorce. I think in some ways that made it

harder to understand, especially at six. I'm still not sure why they got divorced."

"I guess I'm not really clear on that either. I know Dad was distant and grumpy back then. Remember how crazy he was about locking the doors all the time?"

"Oh yeah, I remember," Regina said suddenly as she added a forgotten piece to her memory. "It didn't seem like a big deal then but now it seems really strange. I remember waiting for Mom to get home so I could have someone to talk to."

"Yeah, Dad wasn't much of a talker. That's for sure." They both laughed for a moment, lightening the mood a bit. Now that they were talking about it, it became clear that neither one of them had a clue about what went wrong back then. They talked about their parents' divorce for a while comparing what few things they remembered as young children, sometimes laughing, sometimes feeling sad.

"I wonder what ever happened to that doll." Regina was still holding the mantle doll. "And what's with this strange yard sale, anyway?"

She listened as her sister told a crazy story about an old woman and a yard sale. If the vision hadn't just happened to her, she'd have serious questions about her sister's sanity. As it was, the whole thing seemed barely believable.

"Now that I'm talking about it, I'm wondering if it really happened that way or if I just made it up somehow." Marybeth was shaking her head.

"Well, let me tell you," Reggie jumped in. "What just happened to me was absolutely real, for sure, just like all those years ago."

"I'm really glad you had a vision too. It means that if I am crazy, at least you're crazy with me. And I can't

think of anyone I'd rather go to the loony bin with."
They both laughed for a moment, appreciating the
humor.

"It's funny what the woman in the vision said years
ago. 'This is your job in this life, little one, to help your
sister and others to laugh.' I remember it clearly now.
You know, recently I have started to recognized how
much I enjoy helping people to see the humor in things.
It doesn't take much for me to get on a roll about
something. Tony thinks I should try my hand at stand-
up comedy."

"Really?"

"Well," Regina said apologetically, "It's not like
we talk a lot these days."

"Yeah, I know."

They sat in the living room well into the afternoon
and long past the bottom of the coffee pot. They
eventually got to the sandwiches but not before some
serious damage was done to the cookies. Marybeth
talked more about the bizarre yard sale and the old
woman who was giving things away. Recent events
were seriously challenging her no-nonsense approach to
life. She was much like her dad in that way, they
agreed, concrete, tangible. Suddenly, since just
yesterday, things are more like the way her mother saw
the world.

Oddly, the mysterious yard sale had brought them
crashing back together in a common yet uncommon
experience. Regina asked if she could have the doll.
Marybeth remembered the words of the old woman.

"Yes, I'm done with it," she said, and somehow she
knew it was true.

Chapter 6

Josh unlocked the door to his mother's house and let himself in. The silence was deafening. He wandered through the house, tears welling up in his eyes at every turn. There was her favorite reading chair with a small book case that doubled as an end table. She always had more than one book going at one time. He never understood how she did it. And there was her favorite piece of art over the fireplace. It was a painting done by a local artist a hundred years ago of Pomroy's town common. It included this house back when cars were a rare sight. That and a few other items were included with the house when she bought it twenty years ago. He knew this would be difficult. He thought he had braced himself for it, but now realized the foolishness of his thinking. After all, they had just buried his mother two days ago near his home in Connecticut.

His brother, Rick, told him there was no rush but he felt a need to be here among her things. He needed to attend to her personal things while Rick dealt with the paperwork from his home in New York. A division of labor, if you will, that worked for both of them. Rick had family and couldn't afford the time away in Pennsylvania. In truth, paperwork was more his inclination anyway.

He made his way through the house feeling a bit overwhelmed by the task at hand. When he turned the corner into the den, he spotted his mother's laptop computer set up just where she had left it. They had been video chatting with each other when she fell. He recalled the conversation vividly. It had played over and over in his head a thousand times.

"Hello dear" came the sweet delicate voice of his mother over the ether. "How are things going? Did you finish that article you were working on?"

"Yup. Finished, edited and published in the November issue of Life As We Know It," he replied from across the kitchen.

"Great. Congratulations. I haven't heard of that magazine before. Is that a new one for you?" she asked

"Yes. I came across it at one of the local bookstores recently. It leans toward the spiritual side of life."

"Wonderful. I'll have to pick it up." She enjoyed reading his articles no matter what the content. "Now you can work on your next book"

"Yes, mom" he said. Josh let out a sigh at this familiar conversation.

He paused his memory for a moment to reflect on the first (and only) book he had written. It was a collaborative effort with his girlfriend Jan. They both worked hard on it and the book turned out fabulously.

The relationship with Jan, however, had ended painfully and the idea of starting a similar project gave him a bit of a queasy feeling.

"Books take a lot of work, mom" he pointed out.

"I know. But that's not why you don't write one."

"Yeah, maybe." He knew she was right. She usually was.

"Have you met any interesting women?" was the next question. Again, a familiar conversation between them.

"No, mom. Have you?" he replied jokingly.

"It wouldn't matter if I did. You'd find some reason to eliminate her before you even called her." Right again. "None the less," she went on "the cards this morning said you are going to meet a new love, the Two of Cups, a lovely card about soul mates."

"Anything's possible," he said. He always took her words seriously. He knew his mother had a gift for reading the cards and he had appreciated her insights over the years. This time though, it certainly seemed unlikely. "But right now – nothing's cooking and I don't know that I'm up for a relationship right now anyway". He hadn't been interested in a relationship since the one with Jan had exploded. "I'll keep my eyes open though."

"As will I," she said with a grin.

"The cards also said that you would be experiencing a loss soon." Josh felt an immediate twinge in his gut. His mother was old and despite her good health, he knew, sooner than later, her walk on earth would be over.

A phone rang in the background. "Sorry," she said. "I have to get that. I'm expecting a call." As she got up, Josh saw her stumble. He heard her hit the floor with a sickening thud.

"Mom?! Mom?!" he yelled frantically into the computer.

Instinctively, he had called 911 momentarily forgetting that he was in Connecticut and she was in Pennsylvania. Thankfully, the operator had connected him quickly with the local emergency line in PA and an ambulance arrived within minutes. Josh had stayed on the computer and was able to talk to the medics when they arrived. She was conscious when they loaded her into the ambulance and admitted her to the hospital in Philadelphia.

In the hospital, things had gone from bad to worse. Within four weeks, his mother was gone. And here he was, walking through the things that had made up her life. Thinking about getting rid of them took his breath away. He wondered how anyone ever did this.

Where would he even start? He had seen signs

from time to time for estate sales and wondered if that was the way to go. He knew he couldn't pull it off himself. There was a secondhand shop on the other side of the town common. Maybe they could help him out. He made a mental note to stop by the store later that afternoon.

Chapter 7

The drive to work was easy and familiar, a predictable fifteen minutes under almost any conditions. The small town environment of Pomroy wasn't effected much by traffic or weather. It had become a little bedroom community for those who didn't mind the hour-plus commute to Philly but they were usually gone by 7 a.m.

With a population close to 8,000, Pomroy had just enough of a business district to warrant the one traffic light. The center of town had a bed and breakfast, a hiking and biking shop, a country store that carried a little bit of everything, and possibly the smallest post office in the country. The traditional town common, with half a mile of manicured lawn, and picturesque country roads brought people out from the city on long weekends and for summer vacations. Her shop was located on the corner of Main St. and Westfield Rd., which was the major intersection in town and at one end of the green space.

One Woman's Junque, had taken off unexpectedly and now she was busy most days either in the store or in her garage workshop. She knew her business was allowing her to stay just on the edge of life, like watching the game from the bench. It afforded her long days alone either working on items or out yard saleing. The store gave her impersonal contact with others and a connection to the community. She knew this wasn't the way she wanted to spend the rest of her life, but it served her for the moment.

She recalled the conversation with her sister from the day before as she drove into work, smiling when she remembered them laughing together. Until yesterday, she hadn't noticed how laughless her life had become. Her thoughts shifted to her sister's visions, not only the one from yesterday but the one from thirty years ago, that had bonded them together without either one really knowing it.

The whole weekend had been peculiar and Marybeth was still trying to sort it out.

"Let's see," she said out loud. "A yard sale that wasn't really a yard sale. Four items that I didn't actually buy and one already gone."

She wondered about the ones that were left. The music box that played her wedding song, the family photo and the religious book.

"What next?" she thought. The music box had been next in the line-up and the vision of her wedding. She tried not to think too much about her marriage, not seeing any point in belaboring the past. What would it get her? This music box, however, seemed to have another plan. Fortunately, she was pulling into the alley behind her store and could no longer indulge in deep retrospection.

"Thank God" she thought.

As she opened the back door to the shop she heard a woman call out "Hey, MB is that you?" It was Angie. Marybeth had hired her a year ago to help out.

Angie kept the store open on weekends while Marybeth was out yard saleing and she worked a few hours during the week while her kids were at school.

She took the part time job when her youngest started kindergarten last fall. Initially, she planned to take the summer off, but found that she enjoyed the job and the company of another adult. As a single mom, Angie found it challenging to find adult conversation most days and came to appreciate how important it was to her sanity. She had never married her children's fathers. She took a bit of pride in that. Her choice of boyfriends and birth control might not have been so great but at least she didn't compound it with marriage!

Immediately upon employment, Angie had decided that the name Marybeth was just too long to say, and a bit old maidy, if you asked her, so she stated shortening it to MB. Marybeth didn't much care either way and looked at it as an opportunity to try on something different. Angie was a bit of a character and Marybeth resigned to roll with it.

"How'd you make out this weekend?"

Marybeth paused for an imperceptible moment, memory of the The Box still fresh in her mind. She was not at all ready to talk about the strange events of the weekend and she knew bringing up the shelter would shift Angie's attention. "Great. Got some interesting stuff for the store and hit the jackpot for the shelter."

"Super great." She admired Marybeth for her compassion for the women there and her ongoing support through donations of household goods. Her sister had spent some time there trying to get out of an abusive relationship. It was a tough time and she was grateful to have their services available.

Angie looked Marybeth up and down, noticing her slightly disheveled appearance.

"What happened to you?" she blurted out.

Marybeth smiled a bit and said, "It's been a week-long weekend."

"In a good way or a bad way?"

"I don't know yet. So far, so good I guess."

Marybeth was relieved that Angie didn't push the issue and the two of them commenced emptying the car of the new inventory. Marybeth had a system in the back room of the shop. At least she liked to think she did. On this day, as she looked around, she realized it wasn't working very well. Nonetheless, they unloaded the car and sorted as best they could between those things that needed a little cleanup before they hit the shelves and those that could go right out. Even the things that could go right into the store needed to be labeled, priced and inventoried. The latter being Marybeth's responsibility.

She used a simple inventory/accounting program on her laptop to keep track on things. The cash register was connected wirelessly to the laptop which modified the inventory listing as things were sold. She loved technology and was determined to stay ahead of the rapidly moving curve. Angie, exactly her opposite on this topic, avoided most of the new technology. She didn't even have a cell phone. When she asked Angie about it, she waved her off saying it was just too much trouble and she didn't really need one anyway. Marybeth suspected there was more to the story but didn't push it. She figured if people wanted you to know something, they would tell you.

She was stocking the shelves with the new items when she heard the tingle of the wind chimes that hung over the shop door. She turned to see a well-dressed man in his forties. Definitely not her typical customer. She pegged him for a salesman.

"Hello, are you the owner?"

Yup. Salesman. She wasn't in the mood.

"Depends," she replied. "Are you buying or selling?"

"I'll take that as a yes," he nodded slightly. "And it depends."

"Depends on what?"

"I'm interested in talking about a business proposition."

This was sounding more like a salesman every minute. "Look. If you are selling insurance or advertising or just about anything else, I'm not interested." She put the air of finality on it with a wave of her hand.

"No, no. Not selling anything." He backed up with his hands raised in surrender, the grin on his face revealing two charming dimples. She almost smiled back before her irritable nature took over.

"Did I say something to amuse you?" she asked flatly.

"No, not at all," his grin broadened out to a full-on smile. "I just realized that's exactly what I sounded like. No, it's nothing like that."

"Oh? Then what's it like?" She was skeptical and getting a little rude. She didn't have time to be dragged into an extended conversation by a flirty salesman that she wasn't going to buy anything from anyway.

"My mother owned a house at the other end of the common. I need to empty it of its contents and I can't even begin to think about how to do it." He winced a bit as he spoke. "I thought maybe I could hire you to help me go through things, identify what might be a collectible or antique, then have an estate sale."

"Why would you want *me* to help you with that? Don't you want an auction house?" She was busying herself behind the counter to avoid eye contact.

"Well, for starters, I don't think there are a lot of antiques in the house. Mostly I just don't know what resale value is for anything. Seeing how you're in the business, I figured you would be a good one to help me. And you seem like an honest person who will call it like it is."

"Oh really? You don't know me and you have no idea if I'm honest or not."

"I don't know you, but I've asked around town. You have a good reputation. And I can get a good sense of people."

"Oh, really. And how's that? You have some special talent for it?" she countered.

"Well, actually I do. I see auras," he explained reluctantly, shuffling his feet a bit.

"Auras?" Marybeth asked, only half interested.

"Auras are the electromagnetic fields surrounding everyone's body. I can actually see them. Your aura suggests you're an honest person, uncomplicated."

"Well, stop staring at my auras," she blurted out. Oddly she felt very exposed. This turn in the conversation made her think again about her weird weekend. Had she "caught" some strange bug or fell down the rabbit hole into Wonderland?

"Sorry," he said. "It's not something I can turn off." He held out his hand "My name's Josh Anderson. My mom owned the red Victorian house at the other end of the common."

She shook his hand reluctantly wondering what else he could do besides see auras, whatever that was.

"Marybeth Collette," she said as she shook his hand. "Nice to meet you."

"Likewise," he replied. "Marybeth. That's a name

you don't hear much these days."

"Some people call me MB," she offered almost shyly. She figured what the heck, try it on.

"Okay, MB. So what do you say? I can pay you by the hour with a commission on the estate sale."

Marybeth couldn't argue that it was a sweet offer. Her years of yard saleing had given her an idea of the secondhand value of things and although she was not an antique or collectible expert, she prided herself on identifying things of higher value. It wasn't her main interest though and when she spotted such a thing at a yard sale, she would let the seller know that they might want to have a dealer look at it.

"So Josh, (she used his name with a fake sense of familiarity) when are you thinking this is going to happen?"

"Well, MB" he replied, "I was hoping for a weekend in the fall when the leaf peepers are at a high."

Leaf peepers was a slang term for those city people who drove out to the burbs when the fall colors were at their most magnificent. Marybeth understood this need. Fall was her favorite season by far. She was always stunned by the majesty of nature at this time of year when the trees gave up the glorious colors they had been hiding all summer, like wonderful secrets revealed. These days (After Divorce) autumn brought a comforting urge to settle down for the winter with indoor projects and hot cocoa.

"The Jack-O-Lantern Festival is the third weekend in October. How about then?" Marybeth proposed.

"Does that mean you will do it?" Josh asked with a bit of excitement in his voice.

"Yeah. Why not."

They spent the next thirty minutes hashing out the

details. $30 per hour and 25% commission, pending final approval after Marybeth visited the house. She was cautious to avoid taking on some hoarder's nightmare. They both felt it was fair and Marybeth made plans to visit the house this weekend when she was out and about yard saleing. Josh left her with the address and out the door he went.

Suddenly a hushed voice came from behind her.

"OMG, MB!" She turned to see Angie in the doorway to the back room speaking in code and hand gestures.

"That man was EEAASSY on the EYES, honey. Wooo Wooo" she was saying waving two fingers from her eyes to the closed shop door and back repeatedly.

Marybeth couldn't help but smile back at her and shake her head. Truth was, she hadn't noticed. Was she really that far gone? She had developed a healthy skepticism about men and hadn't had much interest in relationships in a while. As much as she avoided relationships, her ex seemed to embrace them, hopping from bed to bed all over town. It was embarrassing to say the least. She pretended she didn't know about it and everyone else in town did the same. Nonetheless it was painful the way he moved on, and on, and on. She pushed the thought out of her mind. She'd been down that road before and new it would be unproductive.

"I hadn't noticed." She replied.

"Are you dead, girl?" Angie shot back.

"Could be" Marybeth replied wanting to avoid this conversation. "But at the moment I'm happier that way."

"You can't avoid men forever, you know," Angie challenged.

"I'm betting that I can. Now, why don't you help

me with the purged items. I haven't had a chance to take them out of inventory."

"Sure thing, MB," Angie replied.

Every month, they cleared the shelves of items that had been there for more than ninety days and included them in the delivery to the shelter, figuring that the universe was getting things where they needed to be. This new-found go-with-the-flow attitude was new for her, AD, and she didn't claim to have any deep understanding of things mystical. Now she was wishing she had given it a little more thought. What forces, if any, were messing up her perfectly predictable life and why? Not only did she have magical objects in her possession but now Aura Reader had shown up on the scene. What next? She made herself a sticky note to ask Google later about aura reading.

Chapter 8

S he looked at the clock. 2:00 a.m. Grrr. She punched the pillow and rolled over.

2:25 a.m. "Damn!" She grabbed the covers tighter around her.

3:05 a.m. "AAARRRGGGGGGHHH!" She threw the pillow at the clock and groaned.

Tired and grumpy, she got up with a growl. Instead of staring at the clock, she figured she might as well get up and do something productive until the elusive sandman came by again. Turning the light on in the living room and she looked around. So, now what? Not surprisingly, The Box was the first thing to pop into her mind.

She headed to the garage, grumbling under her breath, and brought the box into the living room without incident. She set it on the floor near the couch. The music box rested on the top. It was lightly wrapped in tissue paper with the heads of the wedding couple poking out the top. She didn't really want to deal with this.

"How many times do I have to hash this out?" she asked the couple, shaking her head. "The result is always the same." Somehow she knew she had to do it.

"Okay, okkaaaay!" she was almost yelling now, irritated with the imagined response of the porcelain participants.

"Ripping the scab off yet again."

With a slight tremor, she reached down and touched the music box. Nothing happened. She unwrapped it and sat it on the coffee table. She stared at it. *They* stared back at her, the couple dancing, all smiles and joyful.

"What are you staring at?" she asked them.

She half expected a response. Nothing unusual happened. There they stood, staring back at her. She waited. Nothing. Maybe she needed to do something like meditate or chant. Or maybe there was a magic word.

"Abracadabra," she said, waving her fingers like a magician.

Still nothing. She remembered the song it had played when she first had picked it up. It was the song she and Eric had danced to at their wedding. A Kiss to Build A Dream On by Louis Armstrong. As she thought about it now, it seemed a bit ironic. She had indeed built a rather large dream, fantasy even, on something as fleeting as a kiss. She knew getting married was her own fault, after all there had been warning signs that things were not right. Even up to the week of their wedding she was having quiet doubts. But it seemed impossible to back out by then. Irresponsible, over-emotional, irrational, wedding nerves. She used all manner of denial to get through the day. It seemed ridiculous now but the biggest pressure of all was that she didn't want to look silly or be embarrassed in front of family and friends. Really? Who gets married to avoid being embarrassed?

Although she took responsibility for getting married in the first place, she quickly assigned blame for everything else to Eric. Her fault, she determined, was her desire to believe in the man and the fantasy, ignoring those parts of reality that didn't fit the picture. Eric kept her fantasy alive for years with unfulfilled promises.

She shifted her attention to the music box. She knew the key to this item's story was in the music. Fighting off all her survival instincts, she wound it up. Just before she released the key, she noticed the clock, exactly 3:20 a.m.

She set it down on the coffee table and let the music begin. As she started listening to the familiar song, her head started to spin, slowly at first then picking up speed. "Here we go," she thought.

* * *

The next instant she was deposited in an unfamiliar apartment. She heard voices, a man and a woman drunkenly exchanging insults. When the scene came into focus, she found herself in the corner of a living room watching two adults argue. Gratefully, they seemed oblivious to her. The scene itself however was escalating quickly in both volume and hostility. The man threw an empty beer can against the wall and bellowed, "Eric! Eric! Get your stupid ass in here and help your mother! She's falling down drunk again!" Marybeth found this to be an odd observation from a man who was only marginally better off himself. Suddenly she knew where she was. This was the childhood home of her ex-husband.

A tiny Eric peeked around the corner, eight years old and scared, really scared. He slunk into the room, trying without success to go unnoticed. Eric's father continued his verbal tirade in the drawl of the inebriated, shouting insults at both Eric and his mother. Eric, little as he was, helped his mother to the back room, presumably the bedroom, while dad flopped down on the couch to finish his beer.

Then the scene changed and Marybeth was at a school gymnasium watching a basketball game. She could see Eric on the court, and hear Eric's drunken dad in the stands yelling insults at him.

"What's wrong with you? You shoulda had that!"

Marybeth recognized the drunken drawl from the previous scene.

"I dunno why the coach even lets you play!" A couple of the other parents tried to quiet him but to no avail. Eventually everyone moved away from him on the bleachers. Then, to Eric's horror, the police came and escorted him out of the building, but Eric's dad didn't go quietly. He screamed obscenities all the way out. Eric stood on the court paralyzed, all the color drained from his face. Eric said he had no friends at school but he hadn't said why. No friends outside of school either, unless you counted the kids down the block that he had started to drink with. Then the scene began to change again.

"No more," Marybeth pleaded, to whom she wasn't sure, but the visions were not over. She saw Eric as a young man of twenty-four or so. He was drunk and getting into his car with a young woman. Marybeth held her breath and braced herself. Although she didn't know this part of Eric's life, she certainly could guess this was not going to end well. There was a brief argument about who would drive. The woman seemed to be less intoxicated than Eric, but Eric refused to yield the keys. She watched as the young woman, about Eric's age, got into the passenger side of the car. Off they drove into a dark rainy night. Marybeth *was horrified as she watched the crash that killed the young woman.*

* * *

Then she was whisked back through time and space to the living room, exactly where she started, breathing heavily, her pulse racing, just in time to hear the last few jingles of the music box.

"God, please no more of that," she said aloud to a God she wasn't sure was listening.

She looked up at the clock over the fireplace. 3:20 a.m. Surely that can't be! The vision had seemed to go on forever.

She left the music box on the coffee table, got up and poured herself a glass of wine to calm her nerves. Her pulse began to slow but her heart was heavy as she recalled the scenes of Eric's life. She knew some of his history but until this moment she hadn't really understood the pain he grew up with. Eric's family stories had been vague, lacking detail. Even with just these three scenes, she began to weave together a picture of Eric's life she had not imagined before. No wonder he was estranged from his family. His mother died years earlier from a presumed accidental overdose of alcohol and pills. His father had a studio apartment over someone's garage in Philadelphia, and his sister lived in Maine somewhere. He saw his father rarely and his sister not at all, not even a Christmas card.

Marybeth thought about Eric's bad behavior during their marriage and all the earnest conversations they had about making positive changes. Eric made great promises but never managed to pull it together for any length of time. He reluctantly stopped drinking when they started the fertility treatments but she always felt he resented her for that. When he started overspending, it felt like he was getting back at her somehow. She eventually got tired of arguing about it and began a regular practice of purging the house of unnecessary items. Her regular donations to the local shelter had started back then in an effort at clutter control.

For the second time in as many days, she found herself piecing new information into the story of her life, forcing her to change the well-established picture she'd held onto for years. She thought about their failure to conceive a child and wondered what kind of father Eric would have been. Did he ever worry he would become like his own father? Maybe there had been some divine intervention there after all. If there was such a being, micromanaging the lives of humans, he was doing a bang up job she thought bitterly.

And what about her own past? She was starting to understand how Eric's past was always part of their marriage. How much of that was true for her as well? Was she really still angry at her parents for the divorce? She hadn't ever thought about it. She never was a deep thinker, though. That was Regina's department, but it was starting to seem important. She thought about the strange yard sale again. Who was that woman? And what was the point? Why would an old woman care about Marybeth's life?

The second glass of wine was kicking in and she could see the sandman in the distance. She grabbed the fuzzy throw she kept on the back of the couch, curled up and fell asleep.

Chapter 9

The first rays of the morning sun prodded Marybeth awake. Sitting up on the couch, she found herself face to face with the wedding couple, smiling at her from their happily ever after perch.

"Huh. You again," she mumbled. She rubbed her eyes, got up and made coffee.

Emotionally exhausted and sleep deprived, she tried to make sense of last night's vision. What was the point of all this drama? Who was that old woman? And why on earth had she taken these things home with her? She knew they were haunted from the beginning. Why couldn't someone else have picked them up? For a moment, she considered ignoring the rest of the items entirely. Yes, that was it. She would go about her life, just as it was before the yard sale. She would put the items back in the garage and forget about them. Or maybe she could put them in the store and let some other unsuspecting sap pick them up. Even as she was formulating a plan, she knew it was all for naught. Sooner or later she would deal with each item. She knew she would.

But she could at least avoid it for today. She had plenty on the agenda. The store didn't open until 1 p.m. and closed at 5 p.m. Mornings at the shop never made any money, so she used the time to run errands and work on things in the garage. Today she would deliver goods to the shelter. The task came with mixed emotions. Happy she could help, sad that she needed to. She swung by the store first to pick up the paperwork for the donations.

She was surprised to find Angie there on her day off.

"Hey Angie, what are you doing here?"

"I forgot my purse yesterday so I came by to pick it up after I dropped the kids off at school." Angie explained.

"And I forgot the list of items for the shelter yesterday," Marybeth said, offering an explanation for her own appearance.

"Oh, yeah, I saw it on the counter. I'll grab it for you." Angie vanished into the front of the store and reappeared with the list in hand. "Here you go."

"Do you want to come with me? Help unload and say hello to the staff?" Marybeth was fishing for some company. For the first time in a lot of years, she didn't want to be alone.

"No thanks. I've got a long list of my own this morning. Gotta make the most of those school hours you know."

"Yeah, I get it. Lock up when you leave," Marybeth said as she headed out the door.

Angie paused for a moment after Marybeth drove off, taking advantage of a quiet moment in her day. Angie's thoughts wandered to the woman's shelter, prompting a moment of melancholy. She'd thought about it a lot since she started this job. Marybeth's concern for the women at the shelter had made her feel like there was a connection of sorts right from the beginning. It was one of the ways she knew it was the job for her.

Jackie had been dead almost five years and most days it was still hard to believe. More best friends than sisters, they were inseparable growing up. It was just the two of them as siblings, but there were always people coming and going from their house: aunts, uncles and cousins stayed for a few weeks or a few months while other plans were materializing. It was the kind of house where everyone was welcome. Their family was close and everyone was supportive. One big happy family. That's what made the rest of it so hard to believe.

Jackie had been involved in an abusive relationship for two years when she died. It was surreal and horrifying to watch Jackie's boyfriend manipulate and alienate her. First, he convinced her to live with him. Then he convinced (threatened) her to stop talking to family and friends. Angie recalled the slow progression of events. No matter how much she learned about abuse, Angie still couldn't understand how her sister could let it happen.

The details of that night were still vivid in her mind. She received a call from Jackie, which was rare by that time. She hesitated in picking up the phone. She didn't know if she could go through it again with Jackie. Over the last year, it had been a cycle of "please help me" and "I'm going back to him." Angie reluctantly picked up the phone and heard Jackie sobbing.

"Angie, I'm going to the emergency room. I think my arm is broken." Angie was shocked out of her ambivalence. The violence was escalating.

"How are you getting there?" Angie asked horrified.

"I'm driving myself."

Angie didn't have to ask why. She knew Jackie's boyfriend wouldn't lift a finger to help her. That was part of the abuse, she knew now. Make the victim feel as powerless and helpless as possible so they would stay in the relationship.

"Stay where you are. I'll come get you." Angie was half out of her chair and feeling guilty for her initial irritation.

"No, I'm on the way now. I'll let you know what happens."

Angie knew better than to argue. In the last two years, Jackie had closed herself off so much that she was a completely different person. If Angie pushed even the slightest, Jackie would shut her out instantly.

"I'll meet you there. Be careful," was all she could think to say.

Growing up, Jackie had been a kind and generous person, focused on family, friends and community. She had just started college when she met Jerry. Initially, their courtship was romantic and magic. Jerry seemed the ultimate gentleman, just like a fairy tale. He was a charmer. Everyone liked him.

Then it started to get weird, but nothing you could put your finger on. Still, Angie's gut started tightening up about it. Jackie all but stopped calling. If they talked at all it was because Angie initiated it. At first, Angie thought it was part of the new relationship but, as time went on, she suspected something else was going on. Then things became alarming. Jackie would avoid family and her contact with Angie diminished to almost nothing. When they did get together, Jackie was jittery and jumpy, especially when her cell phone rang. If it was Jerry, she always answered immediately and the conversations usually began with an apology for some unknown offense. Jackie became argumentative whenever Angie pressed her about it.

When Angie got to the ER, Jackie wasn't there. She immediately got worried, then angry, thinking that somehow Jerry had convinced her to go back home. "Here we go again," she thought. Then she heard the sirens and a new realization came over her in a slow wave. She knew in her heart before she knew in her head that it was Jackie coming in.

The police said she ran into a bridge abutment. No other cars were involved and there was no known cause. Jackie survived long enough for Angie to say goodbye. The death certificate read "car accident," but Angie always wondered if it was suicide.

Chapter 10

The Jefferson County Women's Shelter served women and children from Pomroy and the surrounding communities. It was more than just a shelter. They also offered counseling, legal aid and re-establishment services to get families into safe homes. The organization had been around for years, adapting to the changing needs of the population. The shelter opened in the 70s when a little too much free love sometimes landed women in what polite people called "a condition." Now, a single pregnant woman can get by depending on her circumstances, but forty years ago it was quite a big deal to be an unwed mother, and the pressure to give your baby up for adoption was powerful. This was one of those places that women would stay until they gave birth.

Marybeth set off a buzzer inside the shelter when she turned into the driveway, alerting the residents that someone was on the property. Theresa, the house manager, came out to meet her.

"Hi, Angel," she called, waving as she came down the back door stairs.

"Hey everyone, our angel's here. Come help unload."

"Hey, Theresa. How's it going?" Marybeth called back.

"More of the same. You know how it goes."

Women started coming out of the house to help unload. Some faces looked familiar. She was sure they'd been here before. Women often made more than one attempt to break away. That was the pattern of domestic violence. On some level, she could understand why women (or men too for that matter) stayed in a bad relationship. Sometimes it's out of fear of one thing or another but sometimes it's the ever hopeful soul that gets stuck waiting for things to change.

Eric had made promise after promise, apology after apology, keeping her in a constant state of waiting for things to get better. In the end she wondered if any of it had been genuine. It was one of those torturous feedback loops she ran constantly in the early days of her divorce. It had nearly driven her mad. It didn't matter now, she told herself and forced her emotions back in check. She simply refused to go there.

Just in time to pull her out of her own downward spiral, two small children appeared peeking around Theresa's legs.

"Well, hi there." Marybeth was careful not to startle them. "What can I get for you two today?"

"Brian and Sophie," Theresa indicated the children respectively as if she were naming her right leg and then her left, "were wondering if you had any toys they might like."

"As a matter of fact, I think I do. Let's take a look." Marybeth turned to her open hatch and pulled out a box of children's toys.

"Look what I have here." She pulled out a teddy bear in blue jean overalls with tools stuck in the pockets. "What do you think about that, Brian?"

Brian came gingerly out from behind Theresa's leg long enough to accept the toy and then dashed off to the house. Marybeth turned her attention to Sophie.

"Now, let's see. You look like a fairy princess kind

of girl. Am I right?"

Sophie nodded enthusiastically.

"Well, then. I think this might be just perfect." She pulled out a Belle doll in nearly perfect condition.

"What do you think?"

The young girl accepted it, murmured a quiet thank you and darted back to the house after Brian.

"You are a special person, Marybeth. Really, an angel." Theresa hugged her.

She was reaching for the last box to hand it off to Theresa when she continued.

"Marybeth, the shelter's in trouble."

Marybeth turned to her from the open car.

"What do you mean, in trouble?"

"Apparently, one of the board members died recently and they need to fill the spot or else we close."

"Can't they just ask someone?"

"They have. So far, no takers. We were thinking maybe you would take the spot."

"Oh, no way. Sorry Theresa, but I don't know anything about that stuff and I intend to keep it that way."

"No one cares about the shelter the way you do. You are truly an angel."

"I think you're seriously misinterpreting my tax deduction motivation."

"Please Marybeth. Won't you at least consider it. Please, please."

"I'll chew on it a little bit but it's not likely. I'm sure someone will step in."

"I hope so. Anyway, thanks a million as always."

Marybeth handed off the box of toys, closed up the hatch and drove away, waving to the children watching her from the window.

As she drove away, she considered her next stop. There were a few things at the shop that needed minor repairs or clean-up before they could be resold and paperwork was piling up. At the house she had a garage full of works-in-progress. And The Box was there. She considered, with more than a little frustration, how much of her mental energy that thing was chewing up. Whenever her brain had a spare moment, there it was. It was quickly becoming a pain.

The other thing that had started taking up space in her head was Josh. She was curious about him. How coincidental that he should show up with some strange psychic ability just when all this weird stuff was going on. Was that another piece to the puzzle that started with the old woman and the yard sale? Did this all fit together somehow? She started to feel manipulated by the old woman. Who *was* she!? Marybeth felt her frustration level rising. Well, she would not be manipulated by anyone. She resolved to be cautious where Josh was concerned.

When she got back to the shop and opened up her laptop, she noticed the sticky note she had written herself after her strange conversation with him, reminding her to look up aura reading. Marybeth loved all the new technology and the unfathomable amount of information that was right at her fingertips at any moment. Sure enough, her online search netted a long cache of possible websites. There at the top was Wikipedia. She especially loved Wikipedia, so she started there and then clicked on a few other sites to get a variety of information. She learned that aura refers to the energy field around any object or being and is the phenomenon depicted in religious art as halos. In recent times it was more likely considered as nonsense than taken seriously. Now, technology could actually photograph the unseen energy in various colors and wavelengths. Some theories attribute different emotions to each color. Other practices used the auric field to determine imbalances in emotional or physical health. To her surprise, there were "how to" pages in case she wanted to learn how to see auras. The whole idea made her a little nervous. She was already more entrenched in strangeness than she could handle. She wasn't about to go looking for more. As it happened it was time to open the shop, so she closed out the pages and shifted her attention to something she already knew, business.

Chapter 11

Back home that evening, Marybeth considered what to do with the music box. Was she done with it as she was with the doll she gave to Regina? Was there more to glean from it? Somehow it didn't feel done. She decided that it could sit where it was on the coffee table for now. Truth was, she wasn't sure she wanted to touch it again. She eyed The Box, still beside the coffee table from the night before. Leaning over, she peered into it.

The next item from the mysterious yard sale was the family photograph. It occurred to her that her mother's family had the same makeup. Two parents and five kids with her mother as the middle child. Her mother's parents, Grams and Gramps, had been happily married for fifty-three years. Her parents had made it a whopping eight years and her own "till death do us part" had almost come down to that after ten.

For the first time she wondered what life had been like for her mother as a child. It felt a little weird to think about it. Aside from a family portrait that sat on Grams bookshelf, she couldn't recall seeing pictures. What had her mother's life been like? Was she a happy child? Did she get good grades in school? She knew very little about her mother's life. Her family wasn't the kind to tell stories and Mom certainly didn't talk about it much. Mom and Grams had their share of disagreements, though. That much was clear. Marybeth never thought to ask why.

Lost in thought, she absentmindedly reached down to pick up the photo. As soon as her hands touched it, her brain snapped on.

"Oh, shit," she said out loud.

Immediately she was hit with the now-familiar sensation that reality was about to change and, sure enough, it did.

* * *

Marybeth found herself in a room with women of all ages. Most were knitting or crocheting. Four women were chatting quietly in a corner. There was a quick knock at the door, and in rushed a very pregnant young woman. It was her Grams. She was sure of it.

"I'm sorry I'm late," she said as she rushed to an empty chair and pulled out a knitting project that appeared to be a scarf. "The doctor was running a little behind. Jeanie Downs had her baby yesterday, a girl." As she settled down, she noticed a somber tone to the group. She looked around noticing four women sitting in the corner.

"Oh, noooo," she gasped, and color began to drain from her face. "Not Billy too?"

She ran over to the group and put her hand out for the letter one of the women was holding.

United States Army
Casualty Notification Department
Washington, DC

Dear Mrs. Albertson,
Regretfully, this letter is to inform you of the death of your son, Private First Class William James Albertson, who made the ultimate sacrifice for God and his country, in Korea, on February 23,

1951. We offer you and your family our unending gratitude and condolences for your loss. Your family member's remains will be arriving in the United States sometime in March. You will be contacted by our Department of Family Services with more details.

> *In service to a higher good,*
> *General Matthew Stone*
> *Secretary of the Army*

* * *

Marybeth was a little dizzy as her awareness returned her to her living room. Her cheeks were wet with tears and she thought for a moment what it must be like to get such a letter. She considered the current conflict in the Middle East. Communication was so different now. Most of the soldiers had cell phones and internet service. She couldn't imagine the military still used letters to convey a soldier's death. Maybe they sent them anyway, like a sympathy card or a paper record of someone's service.

She looked down at the family portrait in her hand. What did her grandmother have to do with this picture or the mysterious yard sale? What point was the old woman trying to make?

She thought about what little she knew about her family history. From what she did know, Grams was born 1932. Is that possible? It seemed like a ridiculously long time ago. She heard Grams tell a few stories of growing up during the Great Depression and World War II, with food rationing and scrap metal drives. She had married Gramps when he was a soldier in the Korean War and she raised her children during the Vietnam War. Wow, what a way to mark the events of your life Marybeth thought. It was so radically different from her own personal history. Add the cultural revolution of the 60s and 70s and shake well. Marybeth sat stunned for a moment at the breadth of her grandmother's experiences. Her own mother, too, had seen considerable changes in her lifetime.

Knowing this would require a visit to her grandmother, she mentally made room in her schedule that week for a drive into Philadelphia. The whole idea started to make her a little nervous. What was she supposed to say?

"Hi Grams. Have you ever knit a scarf? I saw this vision of you when I picked up an old picture that I found at a very strange yard sale."

Okay, not likely. Heck, it barely worked for her, and she's the one it happened to. She would have to think of some contrived reason for a sudden visit. It would have to be a good one. Grams was old, but still sharp as a tack.

Chapter 12

Marybeth hesitated for a moment then, taking a deep breath, she pushed the last number on her phone.

"Hi Grams", Marybeth said as Grams picked up at the other end. "It's me, Marybeth."

"I know who it is. I can still recognize your voice," Grams paused a moment, then added, "Caller ID helps too. Is anything wrong?" Grams sounded concerned. No wonder. It's not like Marybeth called her regularly...or ever.

"No, no, no. Nothing like that. I just miss you."

"Oh, okay," Grams sounded relieved. "Then when are you coming to visit? I haven't seen you in ages." Marybeth felt bad for the long absence. She hadn't been much for visiting lately. She felt that somehow Grams was disappointed in her for the divorce.

"Thanks for the invitation, Grams. How about tomorrow?"

"Oh." Grams sounded surprised. "Sure honey. Tomorrow will be just fine. (pause) How about lunch? I can make your favorite cheese steak sandwiches."

"I can't think of anything I'd rather do," she said and they laughed. "I'll bring some dessert."

"And to what do I owe the honor of this visit?"

"Well, I'll be honest, Grams" (the first lie), "I have been feeling a bit nostalgic lately and I thought I would put together a photo album of the family with a few stories maybe," (the second lie). Marybeth was afraid the last part might push credibility to the edge. She considered saying 'scrapbooking' but she knew absolutely no one would believe that!

"Ah, you have questions do you?" Grams saw through her in a millisecond.

"Stories and photos. That's all. So dig out some of those old albums, and let's have a look at history. What do you say?"

"Sounds delightful. I'll have a pot of coffee on."

Marybeth hung up the phone. Okay, what now? She hadn't considered this story much beyond the whole nostalgia thing and wondered how far she would have to take it. She hated lying. Mostly because she wasn't very good at it. She'd visit Grams tomorrow and hope for inspiration.

Chapter 13

Timing her drive to arrive just before noon, Marybeth began the journey to Philadelphia just after 10 a.m. Grams had lived in the same old row house for as long as she could remember. The familiar drive into the city felt comforting. She noticed, with a bit of sadness, that a lot of the open space she remembered as a child had been developed into everything from apartment buildings to shopping centers. Struck by the amount of change in just her lifetime, she wondered for a moment what it would be like when she was Grams age, seventy-eight. How would she look back on the events of her own life? With joy? Resignation? Satisfaction? Would she still be angry at Eric? The idea sounded ridiculous and yet, here she was, just as bitter two years out.

Long-exiled emotions were starting to sneak back into her life from the far reaches of her consciousness. She couldn't remember when she started banishing them there but life did seem easier without them. Why were they resurfacing now when things were going along just fine? She cursed the old lady at the yard sale, believing her somehow responsible. Or was she just used to blaming others?

As she got further into the city, where the potential for new development was limited, the landscape remained almost untouched. She was happy to see the Italian bakery was still on the corner. When they were kids, Grams would give her and Regina each two dollars and send them to the bakery to buy something sweet. They always brought Grams back a few green and pink cookies. She planned on continuing the tradition.

The smell of meat cooking greeted her as Grams opened the door. Sure enough, steak was on the grill and cheese was melting. The aroma elicited delightful childhood memories. She and her sister often spent Saturdays with Grams after their parents split up. Mom would be working and Dad had something else to do. Anger crept in at the memory. She suspected that he met up with another woman on those days. He never said, of course, but she would smell a faint hint of lady's perfume on him when he came to pick them up.

"Hi, Grams" she said, giving her a big hug and handing her the box of Italian cookies.

"Well, hello there. Aren't you a sight for sore eyes."

She returned the hug then made Marybeth stand back a moment so she could have a look at her. "Whatever you're doing, honey, keep doing it. You look wonderful." She gave her another hug. "Your timing is perfect. Come on in and sit down. The sandwiches are just ready to come off the grill." Marybeth made her way through the house with ease. It looked just the same as it always did with a few basic upgrades like a new TV and cordless phone. The comfort of familiarity settled her spirit. Even the dishes remained the same. The old radio on the counter played big band music, and for a moment Marybeth felt the walls she had built around herself melt away, revealing the simple joys of childhood.

Lunch was taken up with casual conversation and catching up. Grams had never been to the new store so

Marybeth filled her in on all the details. Grams asked all sorts of questions, wondering how she managed it all. When Marybeth asked about all the senior center clubs, Grams filled her in on the water aerobics controversy (bathing caps vs. no bathing caps), and the upcoming Veterans Day parade. Grams wasn't a vet but Gramps had served in Korean War. He died of a heart attack eight years ago. Marybeth recalled Gramps with a moment's sadness. He was a kind and gentle man as far as she knew, community minded and liked by all. As they were cleaning up the dishes, Marybeth opened a new conversation.

"So, I saw some old photo albums on the coffee table on the way in."

"Yes, I managed to get them down from the top of the closet. I haven't looked at them in years and years. Photos always seem so important when you're taking them but over time we move on and they get put away, like clothes gone out of style."

They were making their way to the living room with coffee and cookies, much like she and Regina had done she noted. That day started out with difficult conversation and ended with visions and stories. Marybeth had a moment of panic. What if Grams had some kind of episode like Regina? What would she do? She hadn't brought any of the items in question with her. Still, she would keep a close eye on things.

They sat side by side on the couch in front of the coffee table. Grams said, "Well, I didn't know exactly what you were after so I gathered what I had. Tell me what it is exactly that you are doing?"

"I just got in a mood about our family, and I realized I didn't really know anything about our history. We don't really tell stories or look through photos. So, I thought I would put something together, like a picture history." The story was weak, and as she said it out loud, it got even thinner. Nonetheless, Grams either bought it or didn't seem to care, happy to share old photos and tell stories.

"This is the oldest album I have. I got it when my mother died. It was her family who came over from Ireland. Every one of them came through Ellis Island without any trouble, which was something to be said back then. Sometimes people were stuck there for months. Or worse, sent back." Grams sounded almost proud as she was telling the tale of Marybeth's ancestors and flipping the pages of old photos. The album was more like an old fashioned scrap book. Photos were intermingled with newspaper articles, baptismal certificates, and the like. Items were glued to black paper pages or loosely inserted into the book. The page edges were frayed and the documents yellowed.

Marybeth was impressed with the stories. "Wow Grams. I didn't know your mother came from the old country. And why would someone get sent back?"

"Well, it wasn't always the cream of the crop that boarded the boats from Ireland. Some were sick. Some were criminals. Some didn't have the right papers or enough money."

"Money? You had to have a certain amount of money to come here?"

"The rules changed all the time, but the U.S. Government was trying to ensure that people wouldn't become homeless and drain the already strapped social budget. You needed to have a sponsor and a certain amount of money. I don't know how much."

Grams picked up the next album and started the same process of flipping and talking. "This album is about my family. My mother married in 1910 and started having children right away. As it turns out, she was very good at it." Grams flashed her a cheeky grin. "She had twelve. My oldest brother was the first to be born here in America and what a big to-do they made of him. Like he was some kind of golden boy. I didn't understand the significance at the time. Immigrants back then mostly felt like second-class citizens. Even the ones who got naturalized worked harder to feel like they belonged here. If you were born here, that meant something. No one could take that away from you. I can imagine what it must have meant to them."

As Grams flipped the pages, the photos took on a more somber subject, photos and articles from World War II. "There's my two younger brothers, Paul and Tim." She pointed to two young men in army uniform. "Everyone was just as proud as could be to have *two* men fighting for America. I remember being both terrified and proud when they shipped out."

The next photo was the gravestone of Grams' brother, Paul, in Arlington National Cemetery. Grams finger hesitated over the photo as if reading some memory from its surface. "We all prayed hard back then that our loved ones would come home. It was a torturous time, waiting for any news that your family member was still alive. We got regular letters from both my brothers. We were lucky to hear anything at all. Some families had no news for months, sometimes years."

She paused a moment, looking beyond the photo to some long ago place. 'We called it the *good* war back then. We were fighting for the safety of the entire world and it was an honor to wear a uniform. But a lot of our best young men didn't come back."

"What happened to Paul, Grams? And Tim? Did he make it back?" Marybeth was becoming fascinated by Grams' stories.

Grams hesitated for a moment, lost in thought. "Paul was in Europe. He died in 1944. Tim was in the Pacific when we dropped the Atom bomb. We were all terrified something bad would happen to him. As it goes, he did come home." Grams paused, then reached out for her coffee pausing in silent reflection. Marybeth took a moment to marvel again at Grams' life. She reached for her own coffee, honoring the silence.

As Grams' continued across the page, a photo jumped out at Marybeth. She sucked her breath in. There, in the corner of the page, was a photo of a group of women of all ages – *knitting*. Marybeth almost couldn't believe it. She hesitated a moment, fearing another vision might be coming on. But none came, and it seemed safe at the moment.

"What's this, Grams?" Marybeth asked, trying to cover the excitement in her voice.

"Ah, we were all knitting scarves for the soldiers. Back then, everyone got into the war effort. I think they even gave out the yarn free so everyone could help as best they could. That's me, in the back there. I must have been pregnant." And sure enough, there was the Grams of Marybeth's vision holding up her knitting with both hands and smiling for the picture. Grams was about to go on to the next page when Marybeth all but grabbed her hand.

"I've never seen you knit. Do you do it anymore?" she asked.

"Oh no. I haven't done it in years," she answered with a laugh. "I did it for a few years for World War II and then again for the Korean War. I used to imagine that the scarf I was working on would find its way to your grandfather even though there was no way of knowing who would get it. It helped me get through the time he was gone. I never picked it up again after he got back. It irritated Gramps. I think reminded him of things he was trying to forget."

Marybeth wondered aloud "I don't really know anything about Gramps' service. No one ever talked about it."

Grams paused for a moment. "For all the praying we did that our loved ones would come back alive, we forgot to pray that they would come back whole. Truth is, a lot of men came back changed. Nowadays they call it that PSD thing."

"Post Traumatic Stress Disorder, PTSD," Marybeth interrupted.

"Yes, that's it. And soldiers can get help. Back then, no one understood what the Vets were dealing with. 'Shell shock' they called it when someone was really bad off, but most Vets just kept pushing forward when they got home. A lot of them calmed their demons with alcohol. But that would just unleash other demons. Some men got violent or destructive in one way or another. They didn't know how to cope. Most men just clammed up, didn't talk about it, and shoved memories as far back as they could. No one talked about it much because no one wanted to open up Pandora's Box. Sadly, we used to say that you were doing okay if your husband didn't drink his paycheck and didn't get violent." Marybeth sucked is another breath as she recalled the words of the old woman in the yard only a few days before. *"He didn't hit me and he didn't drink his paycheck."*

Grams went on turning the pages revealing more

uniformed men. "Here's your Gramps. He was a handsome man to begin with, and then add that uniform and mmm-mmmm," Grams' cheeky grin was back.

"He certainly was easy on the eyes, wasn't he," Marybeth said, borrowing Angie's phrase.

"Yes, he was," Grams agreed.

"Was he already in the army when you met him?"

"Oh, no. We met in high school. He was on the rival football team. We had to date secretly until football season was over."

"Wow. You guys took football pretty seriously."

"Yes indeed. It all sounds pretty silly now but we had fun sneaking around and having secrets."

"What was Gramps like back then?"

"He was an amazing young man, good looking, gentle, excited about life. A real catch!" Grams looked more animated than Marybeth had ever seen her. "You know, one night he even secretly slept in our family car in front of the house so he could walk me to school in the morning. He was crazy like that. He already had his orders to report for basic training when we got married. I was pregnant with your Uncle Jim when he shipped out two months later. He didn't even lay eyes on Jimmy until he was nine months old."

"That must have been terrible!" Marybeth commented, unable to even comprehend the situation.

"Yes. Those were very stressful times, waiting to see who lived and who died. Every time the doorbell rang, there was a flash in my heart thinking that this could be the chaplain informing me of some tragedy."

"Oh God, Grams. How did you do it?" "

"I honestly don't know. You know, you just do what you have to." She paused here for another swig of coffee. "I think those knitting groups helped us all support each other now that I think about it."

"But Gramps did come back," prompted Marybeth, hoping to lighten the mood.

"Yes, he did. But he was never the same. He didn't take to drinking or violence, thank God, but he was jumpy and hard to get along with. The stress of a baby, and then four more, was a lot for him. I know your mother was angry at him for a long time. She felt he didn't treat me right and when she got older, she couldn't understand why I stayed with him. But she never knew the man I fell in love with, the man before the war, the man who would cut out of school early to meet me so he could walk me home, strutting like a peacock whenever we were out together."

"Seems unfair of mom to be so judgmental."

"Maybe so, but, you know, your mother came out of the womb opinionated and judgmental." Grams laughed in loving amusement.

"Yes," Marybeth added, joining in the laughter. "I imagine that's true."

Grams turned the page to reveal a new set of pictures. They were family pictures from Marybeth's mother's childhood in the '50s and '60s. There were photos showing family vacations with all the kids, school activities and graduations. There were also newspaper articles about the unrest of the day. Rosa Parks, the Vietnam War, Martin Luther King, John and Bobby Kennedy, Woodstock, Man on the Moon. Marybeth paused, this time to take in the worldview that her own mother was born into. Was her mother a hippie? She realized she didn't know much about her mother's life either. She knew her parents met at a group called Change Now that advocated for social issues. She noticed a clipping that mentioned the group in the title.

"Is this the group where mom and dad met?"

"Yes," Grams smiled and shook her head. "That was the day she got arrested."

Marybeth bolted upright. "What?!"

"You don't know?" Grams asked with mock surprise. "They were handcuffed together around the gate of Arlington National Cemetery."

"What?! Ah, no. Strangely, she never mentioned it." Sarcasm was seeping through the shock.

Grams let out a hearty laugh, clearly pleased with herself for the shock value.

"Your mother got caught up in the unrest of the day, "counter-culture" they were calling it. Thankfully, she wasn't into all the drugs that were going around – at least not that I know of. She was a wild one though, channeling all her anger at anything that got in front of her. She marched on Washington almost weekly it seemed." Grams paused here to smile up at Marybeth and shake her head.

Marybeth was shocked. "Wow. I never even imagined this part of mom."

"There was always something to protest back then but mostly it was the Vietnam War of course and women's rights. Then she married your dad. I think being married to a Vietnam Vet helped her to understand Gramps a little bit more. When she started noticing the same behavior in your dad as she did in Gramps, she divorced him. In some ways she was taking advantage of the new attitudes of the day but also I think it was to prove something to me. Like she wasn't going settle for a bad marriage like she thought I had."

"Wow," was all Marybeth could thing to say. All

this talk forced Marybeth to look at her life and her mother's life in a bigger way.

Grams continued to flip through the pages, into the life and times of Marybeth and Regina. She listened politely but her interest and attention span was waning. They finished the last album simultaneously with the coffee and cookies.

"Did you get whatever it was you were after?" asked Grams.

"And then some," Marybeth replied.

"Do you want to take these with you?" Grams asked with a slight hesitancy, placing her hand gently on the stack of albums.

"No," Marybeth replied. "I'd like to come back another day and make copies of things." Oddly, this time it was the truth. Grams seemed relieved that the albums would remain in her care.

"Okay dearie, give me a call ahead of time. Just because I'm old doesn't mean I'm sitting around watching TV. My schedule can get pretty full."

Marybeth hugged her and promised more of a notice next time. She stopped at the bakery again before heading home. They had the best Boston Crème Pie Marybeth had ever tasted. Or was it just the sweet memories of Grams and Regina that went along with it? It didn't matter. Marybeth took one home planning to call her sister for dessert and to share all Grams' stories.

Marybeth's brain was on fire as she headed out of Philadelphia. She assumed that her grandmother's marriage had been a happy one. After all, it lasted fifty-three years! She also assumed that her own marriage and her mother's had been failures. Now, things looked different. Had Mom really divorced Dad to prove a point to Grams? It was all hard to believe. Had she stayed in her own marriage way past healthy to prove the opposite point to *her* mother? She had a long drive home to think about it.

Chapter 14

It was Saturday again and Marybeth hit the yard sales early with a slight sense of caution considering last week's adventure. She noticed that she looked at things differently now, not only seeing their potential but also wondering about their past. She was a bit more hesitant about actually touching things too, feeling like reality had permanently changed and she wasn't sure of the new rules.

Nonetheless, her car was half full when she turned towards the old Victorian house on the common to meet Josh. It was a beautiful clapboard house, deep red, with a wraparound porch and charming gingerbread accents. The trim was painted in light rose and deep purple perfectly highlighting the architectural detail. It was a mansion in its day with a long manicured front lawn connecting it to the street. The outside at least was well cared for and maintained. Marybeth pulled into the driveway beside a classic light blue Mustang, '65 by the looks of it. She assumed it was Josh's. "Boys and their toys," she thought.

As she walked up to the door, she heard soft music playing from inside. When she rang the doorbell, it had a soothing wind chime sound that was out of character for the house. Josh met her at the door, hand outstretched in greeting.

"Hi. Good to see you again," he said.

Marybeth shook his hand, "Same here," she said, immediately feeling awkward. She was starting to notice what Angie had seen instantly. Josh was a good-looking man, in his mid forties, in good shape, with strong chiseled features offset by a gentle demeanor. She wondered what his aura would look like if she could see it. Why she hadn't seen him around before this? She figured he must be from out of town.

"Come in," he said as she stepped into the foyer. Marybeth braced for disaster. She knew that homes of the elderly had a tendency to become overwhelmed with things that had long since passed their usefulness, cluttering up hallways and spare rooms.

She found herself standing in the typical entryway of old Victorian houses, a sitting room on each side with large wood pocket doors that disappeared into the walls. To her surprise, the house was almost immaculate and tastefully furnished in a way that respected the character of the house. The high ceilings and open foyer gave it a sense of old-time elegance.

"Wow," was all she could manage, again feeling a bit awkward. "Did your mother live alone?"

"Yes, until about a month ago when she fell and broke her hip. She never recovered. She died three weeks ago at a nursing home in Westfield," he replied. The statement hit Marybeth in the gut. Overly involved in her own drama, she had never made the connection the *cleaning out his mother's house* meant something bad had likely happened.

"Oh, God," she gasped. "I'm sorry for your loss. I'm so sorry for not paying more attention. I can only imagine how difficult this must be for you."

"Thank you. No apologies necessary. My mother had a good life, all seventy-nine years of it." Marybeth was a bit surprised thinking of her own mother who was fifty-eight and her grandmother closer to Josh's mom's age at seventy-eight. He picked up on something, maybe her puzzled look, maybe that damn aura thing.

"You're surprised."

"Just thinking of my own mom who is only fifty-eight. How old are you?"

"Forty-six. My mom had me when she was thirty-five. I'm six years younger than my brother. How about you?"

"Thirty-eight," Marybeth replied. "Mom was a tender eighteen when her family started with my arrival. My sister arrived almost three years later."

"My mother obviously started a bit later," he said with a smile. "I know she had a hard time getting pregnant and there were a few losses before and after my brother. The doctors said she wouldn't have any more children. Then she had me. Doctors aren't always right."

Marybeth fell silent, feeling her own pain of infertility. Could her doctors have been wrong too? No. She'd been down that road already, and it only ended in pain.

Unclear how to interpret Marybeth's silence, Josh went on as they wandered slowly though the house. "The whole experience turned my mom's life upside down. She became disillusioned with medicine and religion and started on a search for what she called 'other truth'. Over time she accepted a much more expansive view of reality than traditional religion." Josh caught himself in his own reminiscence. "Oh, I'm sorry for rambling. Somehow I feel like I want you to know her."

"It's fine. Really. I'd love to hear about her." This

statement wasn't entirely true but she felt that Josh needed to tell his story and she didn't mind. After all, she was wandering through this woman's house. It seemed respectful to know her at least a little. She felt a pang in her heart for Josh. It must be difficult to dismantle your mother's home.

"Years ago, she told me she would leave her body before she was eighty and that I shouldn't worry. I'll see her again when I get there."

"Yikes." She immediately put her fingers to her mouth as if to prevent other words from escaping.

Thankfully, Josh flashed her a brief smile. "I'm not going to lie, it creeped me out a little at the time but Mom always talked like that. I didn't even remember the conversation until someone mentioned her age at the funeral." Josh paused at the memory. "But that's probably too much information."

"Not at all," she lied, "I love hearing people's stories." The real truth was, she'd become quite self-centered, consumed in her own grief and unhappy marriage. She thought about Josh's mom for a moment. His mom had used her grief to seek peace and answers. Marybeth had simply stayed angry and hurt, allowing her world to get small and her outlook jaded.

Josh went on, "She had a gentle transition to whatever is next, dying in her sleep. Mom always considered sleep to be the world between here and what's next."

Marybeth realized, in another moment of self-reflection that she never thought about what might be *next*. Josh pulled her out of the thought as he motioned with his hand that they continue further into the house.

"I've been staying here since Mom's fall. Let's go through here to the kitchen." Marybeth made a mental note that he had not been home in almost two months.

In addition to the house being clean, the woodwork was well maintained with wax or oil, the hardwood floors shined, even the windows sparkled. The furniture was high quality and in good condition, with original art on the walls, hard cover books lining the shelves and crystal bowls in the hutch. But the most surprising items were the electronics all over the house. There was a desktop computer with wireless keyboard and mouse. A wireless router that sent internet to a laptop computer in another room. An HD flat screen TV and a stereo system wired throughout the first floor had a central remote that turned everything on and off, including the lights.

"Did all of this belong to your mother?" she asked with disbelief. Grams had barely mastered the cordless house phone they got her for Christmas two years ago.

"Yes," Josh answered laughing. "My mother was a little old gray-haired techno-geek. She loved it all. I'm going to have a hell of a time making sure that all her online accounts are closed. She had 183 friends on Facebook!" He shrugged and smiled, shaking his head. "She Skyped with my brother and me regularly."

Marybeth was smiling now too. "She must have been quite a character. I'm sorry I never got a chance to know her. I've lived here quite a few years now but don't remember seeing her at all." Marybeth was starting to realize just how small her world had gotten.

"She traveled a bit and had a small condo in Florida for the winters. She stayed with me or my brother for long visits too," he replied.

They continued to walk around the house, making their way to the kitchen, which was well appointed with three complete sets of dishes, pots and pans galore and kitchen gadgets of all sorts.

"She wasn't as much of a cook as the equipment would imply. It was more like she went with the trends. There was the juicing phase," he indicated a large machine on the counter, "the bread making phase, the smoothie phase, and the 'as seen on TV' grill that drains off all the fat phase." With a Price Is Right wave of the hand and a tender smile, he indicated the required countertop appliance. Marybeth was starting to feel disappointed that she had never met the woman whose home she was now rummaging through with dollar signs in her head. But, after all, that was why she was here.

They returned to the foyer where a long hardwood staircase invited them to the second floor. It had a lovely wood banister with spindle posts, all stained a deep cherry red. The stairway went up three steps to a landing, which displayed a large oil painting of the town common as it must have looked 200 years ago. Then the stairs turned ninny degrees to ascend the rest of the way to a generous second floor landing with two hallways that branched off in opposite directions. Straight ahead was a small room with a deep red curtain draped over the doorway, closing most of the room off from view. They traveled down the each of the hallways, Josh giving a brief description and history of the house and furnishings. His mother purchased the house eighteen years ago and restored it using government funding and grants available to preserve historical buildings. She had overseen all the work herself. Marybeth couldn't imagine ever taking on such a task.

There were a total of five bedrooms, all well-furnished, three baths, a linen closet complete with towels, bed sheets, blankets and comforters, all appearing in good condition. Prefect for the women's shelter. She wondered if Josh would want to donate them. The reality is, linens don't sell well at yard sales, no matter how nice they are. All the other items looked like they would sell out if they held the sale for two full days and advertised it well.

As they came back to the top of the stairs, Josh paused for a moment at the sunroom, then gently pulled the curtain open waving Marybeth into the room. The room had a circular outer wall that made the room larger than she expected. Four tall thin windows with lovely stained glass borders offered an impressive view of the town common. The length of green lawn was punctuated by the tall white bell tower of the Pomroy Congregational Church at the other end. On the wall opposite the windows was a large painting of a gypsy fortuneteller sitting in a wooded glen peering into a crystal ball. It gave Marybeth a bit of a creepy feeling in light of recent events.

In the center of the room was a small round table with two chairs. The table was draped with a lovely silk scarf of rich blues and purples. Sitting on top of the scarf were ten strange looking cards laid out in an odd pattern with the remainder of the deck off to the side. Marybeth wasn't sure why, but it looked important. She realized that this was the only place in the house that contained any personal items and wondered if Josh couldn't bring himself to remove it. "What's this?"

"This was my mom's reading room. We cleared all the personal items from the rest of the house but I just haven't been able to pack this up yet. My mother was a tarot card reader."

"Is that anything like an aura reader?" she asked,

flashing a small smile and only half kidding. Although she had looked up aura reading online, she still wasn't quite sure what it was. All this esoteric stuff was way out of her league and she was still dazed and confused by her own recent experiences.

"Sort of," he replied. "Tarot cards date back at least to medieval Europe, depending on who you ask. They were originally playing cards similar to what we use today. Somewhere along the way, the cards began to be used as a way to divine esoteric information, predict the future in a way or access some information not otherwise known."

A week ago Marybeth would have scoffed at all this as mumbo jumbo but considering recent events, now it seemed a bit more plausible. Her head started to swim with all the events of the past few days. She must have looked a bit off because Josh stepped closer to her, took her arm and said, "Are you alright? You look a little pale."

"A little low on the blood sugar I think."

"Why don't we go downstairs and have some tea."

"Coffee if it's all the same, please," She let him lead her downstairs to the kitchen.

Marybeth took a seat at the kitchen table as Josh approached the counter. Taking on his Price is Right wave he asked, "Standard drip? K cup? French pressed? Or single cup drip?"

She couldn't help but smile. "K cup will be fine. And it's easiest."

"So it is."

Josh pulled a bakery box of cookies out of the cupboard and placed it on the table.

"Help yourself."

"Thanks."

Then turned back to the cupboard looking for coffee.

She smiled at the white chocolate macadamia nut treats. It was her favorite comfort food. She took one without hesitating knowing that the sugar would revive her while she waited for the coffee. Josh stood with his back to her as he worked at the counter. She took the opportunity to look him over. He was a good-looking man. Just tall enough, slender athletic build, nicely dressed. No wedding ring, not that she cared, right?

As she looked around the kitchen she began to notice empty spots on counters and in the hutch indicating that some item had been removed. The walls were mostly bare, with nails and picture hooks holding empty space.

"Did your mother believe in angels and spirits too?" she asked, curious about the upstairs room but not knowing how to ask politely. She felt way out of her element here but hoped that somehow this could help her understand her own experiences.

"To a degree" he said. "Mom believed more in angels here on earth. Do good-ers, you might say. People that uplift others. Mom would tell me about an angel that showed up at a charity she was involved with. A woman that came regularly with donations of clothes and household items for a local women's shelter."

Marybeth froze for a moment with the next bite of a cookie half way to her mouth. "What shelter?" she asked cautiously.

"The one across town for women and children. Mom was on the board of directors. Do you know it? Mom would tell me 'the angel arrived today' or 'we're hoping the angel brings a this-or-that,' and sure enough, the angel would appear with it. We found hundreds of letters of gratitude from. . ."

He turned from the counter to see Marybeth looking more pale than before and seemingly frozen, staring off into nothingness. Her aura was nearly gone and dark red. He didn't always know how to interpret what he saw but he figured this wasn't good.

He rushed over to her "MB, are you alright? What's wrong?"

"It's me," she replied, not breaking her far-off gaze. Her brain struggled to reorganize once again, as she realized the value of what she had been doing just as a matter of course, her nonchalant good deed for the day. She brought what she had and they were always so grateful and kind. Sometimes she wondered if her only real motivation was the uncomplicated kindness that she was shown each time she went, like she mattered to them even though they hardly knew her. She didn't even know most of their names. They called her "Angel."

"What do you mean it's you?" He had knelt down beside her and was rubbing her hand gently between his two.

"It's me," she repeated in a whisper, trying to see herself as this benevolent benefactor that Josh's mom considered an angel. It was a little too much for her. She wondered why her head hadn't exploded yet.

"Have you eaten today?" Josh asked.

"No," Marybeth responded in a bit of a daze.

"We're going get some lunch."

"That would be great" she replied flatly, without protest. Josh attempted to help her up but she shook him off. "I'm fine, really," she lied. She walked a bit slowly, taking a deep breath when she got outside. Josh led her across the lawn to the Mustang.

"Nice car," she commented as he opened the door for her.

"It was my mother's," he replied with a smile. Marybeth was not surprised.

Chapter 15

At first, lunch had that awkwardness of strangers thrown together. They both filled the space by sharing superficial information. Marybeth learned that Josh lived in Connecticut with his cat. His brother lived in New York. As a freelance author, Josh could easily work anywhere so he agreed to handle things on the ground here while his brother did what he could from there.

Marybeth talked about growing up in the town next door. Her mother worked part-time, teaching at the community college. Her dad retired two years ago from the same place. Her sister, Regina, lived just around the corner from her, making the whole family within ten miles of each other.

"No husband and kids?" Josh asked.

"An ex-husband and no kids. How about you?"

"Never married. No kids. My brother Rich is in charge of keeping the family name going with a wife and three children. It takes a lot of the pressure off," He flashed a quick smile. "So, tell me, what's your connection to the shelter?"

"Not as dramatic as you might think, especially considering my overreaction from earlier." She was feeling uncomfortable and a little embarrassed. "I just do what I do."

"And what is that, exactly?"

She explained that her weekly trips to the shelter were as

much practical as altruistic. She'd pick up a few things at yard sales plus get rid of old inventory from the shop. She saw it as a win/win/win.

"I imagine it isn't easy for them. I figure my donations are one small thing I could do to help. That's why it caught me off guard to hear how other people thought of it. It's become sort of a habit for me."

"Well, what you see as a weekly task, others see as a generous and sometimes life-saving act. My mother couldn't say enough about it. It's a little crazy that I got to meet you. It almost feels like my mother's hand is in it somehow." Josh laughed and waved his arms in a comical zombie style that made Marybeth laugh along with him.

"Or it's just a really small town," she added, dismissing the coincidence and at the same time wondering a little herself if there was an otherworldly force at play.

"Well, either way, I'm glad to pass on the gratitude, first hand."

Marybeth was desperate to change the subject. "So, did your mother have siblings?" Marybeth asked, knowing how obvious a move it was.

Josh noted the shift. "Mom was one of five. She had a sister who died when they were kids. Mom didn't talk much about it. A car accident is all I know. The rest lived into old age."

"Are any of them still around?"

"I have one aunt who lives near me in Connecticut. I watch out for her as much as she'll let me, but she's one of those stubborn Yankees. Doesn't want or need help from anyone. So I just do what she tells me to." He was smiling again, a genuine smile that warmed her heart slightly, which brought its temperature from arctic ice to Rocky Mountain snow.

Lunch seemed to go quickly and soon they returned to the house and the business of the day. It was Marybeth now who walked around the house sharing her thoughts about this item or that. There were some art pieces that might bring in more money from an art auction house which might drag things out for several months. The alternative was to invite a few of the local antique experts to a pre-sale to purchase things at wholesale prices.

When it came to the electronics, Marybeth was a little less optimistic. People didn't like to buy used computers and gadgets, afraid of viruses or glitches that could cost hundreds of dollars to fix. "There's a computer repair shop in town that I've used before. They're very good and reasonably priced. Maybe they could somehow guarantee them."

"Thanks. I'll look into it this week."

"What about this?" Marybeth noticed a cell phone on the desk. It was fairly new, one that could check your email and comes with a full key pad. "This would probably sell if. . ." As she picked up the phone she immediately felt the familiar fuzz of a vision and thought *Oh, shit, not again,* just before she slipped into another world.

* * *

As the vision came into focus she saw Angie, in a hospital room, sobbing and angry as she read something on a cell phone. This wasn't right. Angie didn't have a cell phone. In fact, she had an aversion to them. And yet, here was Angie, scrolling down the page, alternately sobbing and clenching her fist in the air just before collapsing into a chair.

* * *

And then, the vision was gone and Marybeth was back in the den of the old Victorian house with Josh, who was once again looking at her with concern.

"MB, are you okay? Is this another sugar moment?" he asked, half joking.

"Yes, no, I mean I'm fine," Marybeth stammered. "I was just remembering something . . . that I forgot that I knew. I'm okay," she lied.

"Do you want to sit down? It has been an exhausting day," he said, gesturing to the sofa and reaching out a hand. "I'm sure you started bright and early with the yard sales."

"No, I'm fine." Marybeth's brain was scrambling, trying to simultaneously come up with an excuse for her behavior and look nonchalant as Josh lead her to the sofa. He sat beside her, looking at her, waiting for an explanation.

"Well," she almost stammered, "sometimes… recently… not that often really. . ." she looked up at Josh who was waiting patiently for her explanation. She hadn't told anyone of the recent events except Regina and that was only because Regina had a similar experience. Marybeth still wondered if they were both crazy. She decided to test the waters here and share a little bit of recent history, feeling somewhat safe with a man who claims to read auras. Still, she was not prepared to go into the whole story, so she kept it simple. She took a deep breath and started.

"I have a very vivid imagination," she began. "Believe it or not," she added when she saw his skeptical look.

"And sometimes I get a sense of some story that might go along with an object." Marybeth knew this was going badly when she looked up at Josh's face. He looked hopeful, waiting for the conversation to make sense.

"Just an over active imagination then?" he asked.

Marybeth knew she was a terrible liar and decided to fall back to the truth, at least some of it.

"Okay. Recently, for some reason that I don't begin to understand, images appear to me from certain objects." There, she said it out loud. And waited.

"And?" Josh replied as if she had done nothing more than comment on the weather.

"And I'm feeling a little weird about it. And when it happens, my first thought is that I must be crazy. Then life goes on as usual, which makes me *sure* I'm crazy and I just don't know it yet."

Still in his 'this-is-all-normal' attitude, Josh asked "And does this have something to do with the cell phone?"

"It just happened again. I got a vision of Angie, my assistant at the shop," she tried to sound casual. "It doesn't make any sense because Angie is a technophobe. She wants nothing to do with cell phones and barely uses email."

"If you think Angie needs to have the phone for some reason, please give it to her."

"Thank you. Don't you think this is all a little weird?"

"Well, I grew up with unusual things happening. Remember? I've been seeing things most people don't see since I was small. I know there's more to life than what meets the eye. So, for me, you having visions is just another way of knowing something."

"Seriously? You must be as crazy as me."

He looked away for a moment. "My mother had a

gift of knowing things," he said as his mind drifted into memories. "Her information didn't necessarily come through objects though. She would refer to it as things she 'just knew.' She used tarot cards to help her clarify information." There was a moment of silence between them before Josh changed the subject. "Alright, MB. Let's finish going through the house." They got up from the sofa and headed out of the room. Almost as an afterthought, Josh turned to Marybeth and smiled, "but don't touch anything."

"Not to worry." Smiling back, she pulled her arms in across her body.

As they headed upstairs, Marybeth resumed her commentary on items in the house. Linens should be bundled together and labeled. Small items should be gathered together downstairs. Customers would have until the following day at noon to pick up larger items. They went through the entire upstairs before they got back around to the room at the landing. They both hesitated a moment before going in. It occurred to Marybeth that this might have been the last thing his mother did before she fell.

Slowly Marybeth continued her commentary once inside. "These will probably sell easily," she said as she reviewed the books on the shelf. They were mostly of a spiritual or esoteric nature and she thought they would sell easily in this new age. "Except for this one, maybe," she was saying as she gently pulled a well-worn book off the shelf. She noticed that Josh flinched ever so slightly as her hand touched the book. At first she thought it was a reaction to her touching his mother's things. As he watched her curiously for a moment, she realized he was worried about another episode of helplessness. She immediately got irritated with him and then with herself. "I'm fine," she said, almost too loudly. Josh, fighting a grin, backed away slightly and raised his hands in surrender without saying a word.

Marybeth's attention turned to the book in her hands. It had a soft leather cover that showed years of use. Although she was not receiving any vision about it, she sensed it was important. For a brief moment, her mind wandered to the prayer book from the yard sale. It seemed similar, but she couldn't put her finger on it. Maybe the same size. The book in her hand was plain blue with one word "Tarot" stamped into the leather on the front. The faint remains of gold leaf could be seen in the deeper edges of the letters. As she flipped through it, she noticed beautiful pictures similar to the cards displayed on the table. "What is this, a guide book?" she asked.

"Yes, although I don't think mom used it much anymore."

Without thinking, she reached down and picked up the next card in the deck. She and Josh both froze for a split second. No vision. Marybeth turned over the card. It was an image of a man and a woman looking at each other, each holding a cup. "Two of Cups" she read. She looked at Josh for some explanation.

He shrugged his shoulders. "I have no idea. It was my mother's thing."

Marybeth opened the book to see what meaning the card held. She read aloud:

"To understand the Two of Cups, all you have to do is look at its image. A man and a woman are gazing at each other, ready to share their emotions. Here is..."

Marybeth faltered a little. Josh reached out for the book, wondering what she was stumbling over, and continued.

"Here is the very picture of romantic and sexual attraction. If you have drawn this card, be prepared for romance." Now he was the one feeling a little awkward. "Okay. I guess that's enough of that." He closed the book and placed it on the table.

After an awkward moment, they both refocused on the contents of the room.

Josh wandered around the little room, touching things gently. "It's as if leaving this last piece of her here in the house means she isn't really gone," he said, putting his hands in his pockets. "I still can't bring myself to move anything."

Marybeth noticed a shift in Josh's demeanor. For the first time, she got a sense of Josh's grief. She said gently "I can pick them up for you if you like. You can decide later what you want to do with them."

"Yes, thank you," he replied quietly without taking his gaze off the table.

He stood very still, watching, as Marybeth collected the cards and placed them with the rest of the deck, being sure to keep them turned in the same direction. Removing the scarf from the table, she placed the cards and book in the center, then folded it around them, securing both items inside.

Without moving, Josh said softly "Interesting. My mother folded them up just like that."

She held the deck out to him.

Without taking his hands out of his pockets, he said "You keep them for now."

"Are you sure? They belonged to your mother."

"I'm sure," he said looking up at her, eyes filling with tears.

Marybeth looked away awkwardly, feeling like

things were suddenly a little too intimate. Inhaling deeply, she broke the moment.

"Okay, I've had enough for one day. How about you?"

"Yes, I guess we both have," he replied. He gestured towards the door and Marybeth preceded him out of the room and down the stairs. They walked through the house in silence. As they got to the front door they agreed to meet up later in the week to plan the last details of the sale. Josh was still standing in the doorway as Marybeth drove off.

Chapter 16

Marybeth headed off to the shop Monday morning as usual. And, as usual, Angie was already there, straightening up after the weekend.

"Good Morning, Angie," she began "How are things going?"

"Good Morning, MB. Great and crazy. The kids are all jazzed up about Halloween. We went shopping for costumes this weekend and things will be in high gear from now till the thirty-first. How was your weekend?"

"Well, I ended up over at Josh's house to get ready for the estate sale." She tried to sound nonchalant.

"Oh, that's r-r-i-i-i-ght," Angie said with a sly smile on her face. "How'd *that* go?"

Marybeth knew the question was not about the estate sale but about her day with Josh. She intentionally skirted the issue. "It's a nice house with lots of nice stuff. His mother died recently and he is trying to clear the place out. He should be able to sell most of it and make a few bucks for his mother's charity. And hey, get this. His mother's charity is the women's shelter."

"Wow, small world. Did you know her?"

"No. She was mostly in the background, on the board of directors. It was interesting to hear Josh talk about the shelter from the other side of things, though. Oh, and I found

something at the house that I thought you might like."
Marybeth reached into her bag for the phone.

On the drive over, Marybeth concocted the story
she would give Angie about the cell phone. She would
say that she commented to Josh that Angie was
reluctant to embrace technology and thought this phone
would be a perfect way for her to cross the line. She
would explain that Josh suggested she take the phone to
Angie. She would take time to show Angie how to use
it. Her plans quickly changed when she saw Angie's
reaction. Angie stepped backward as if the phone might
explode, then stood there staring at it with caution.

"Hey. What's up?" Marybeth asked. "Are you
okay?"

"Fine," Angie replied. "You know I don't like cell
phones. Why would you bring it for me?"

"Just trying to bring you into the new millennium,
that's all." Marybeth smiled slightly trying to lighten
the moment.

"I don't want it, but thanks." Angie made busy
work for herself in the opposite direction.

"Fine, I'll just leave it here and you can think about
it." Marybeth set the phone on the counter as she
headed into the back to unload the car.

Once Marybeth was out of sight, Angie turned to
the cell phone and hesitated, lost in thought. It looked
exactly like the cell phone her sister Jackie had when
she died. Angie's stomach tightened up at the
recollection. Suddenly she understood why she avoided
cell phones. Slowly, Angie walked over the phone and
picked it up.

* * *

Angie felt reality bend and suddenly, she was
transported to a night five years ago as she

watched herself burst through the ER doors. Rushing to the desk, she inquired about Jackie. No one by that name had arrived. Angie called her sister's cell but Jackie didn't answer. She knew something was wrong. It occurred to her that her sister might have turned around and headed back to the degenerate who broke her arm in the first place. Anger took over as she waited in the ER, hoping her sister would show up and get the help she needed both physically and mentally.

Then she heard the sirens. In her gut, she knew they were bringing her sister in. A nurse rushed out from the treatment area to inform the receptionist that an ambulance was arriving.

"We have one coming in. ETA one minute. Jackie Delgato. Car accident. Looks bad." The receptionist immediately picked up the phone and started making calls as the nurse vanished into the back again.

Angie felt panic creeping over her. She ran to the counter. "That's my sister, oh my God, that's my sister," was all she could say.

The ambulance arrived a moment later and the paramedics wheeled her sister into the ER. Angie kept insisting on seeing her but was thwarted every time by nurse guards just inside the doors. Two police officers arrived a few minutes later and began asking Angie questions. Angie related the most recent events, including information about Jackie's abusive boyfriend and where they could find him. The next question caught Angie completely off guard.

"Has your sister ever tried to kill herself?"

"You mean besides living with a brutal sociopath?" Angie spat out before she could stop herself. She remembered the many times she and other family members called the police, sending

*them to Jackie's house during one of her
boyfriend's violent episodes only to have them
walk away saying there was nothing they could
do. For all Angie knew, this was one of those
officers.*

*"Ma'am, we're just asking," the officer said
trying to keep Angie calm.*

"Why are you just asking?" She shot back.

"Ma'am, please answer the question."

"Not that I know of."

*"How did she sound when you talked with her
tonight?"*

*"Really?!" She was furious. "She sounded like
a woman who had the shit beat out of her by a
man who physically and emotionally abuses her
on a regular basis. She sounded like a woman
who had to drive herself to the hospital with a
broken arm because that piece of shit wouldn't
help her. That's how she sounded."*

*"Ma'am, there were no skid marks at the
scene."*

"What are you saying?"

*"It doesn't look like your sister made any
attempt to stop or swerve before she hit the
bridge."*

*"What! What are you saying? That she drove
straight into that. . ." Angie fell silent as she began
to understand what the officer was implying.*

*"Well, if she did, it's your fault!" she spat out.
"How many times did the police go out to her
house and do nothing! Sometimes there wasn't
even a report taken! You all left her there to die!"
Angie was now alternately crying and screaming.
The officers did their best to calm her but the
scene went on until the nurse came out and told
Angie she could see her sister. As she turned to
go, the officer handed her a business card saying*

that she could call if she had any questions.

Angie immediately shifted her attention to the nurse who escorted her into the back area. The nurse sternly cautioned her about upsetting her sister. The doctor met her just outside the room.

"Hi, I'm Doctor . . ." but Angie wasn't listening. She was looking in at her sister, lying in bed, bloody, bruised and unconscious.

"It was a bad accident," the doctor said when Angie finally turned her attention to him. "She has a lot of severe internal injuries. If there are other family members that should be here, you might want to call them."

"What? What are you saying? Is she dying?" Angie asked incredulously, hoping desperately that she misinterpreted these comments.

"She has a collapsed lung, many broken ribs, a concussion, a broken arm and a broken leg that we know of. There's internal bleeding that we haven't located yet. We will be taking her into surgery as soon as we can, maybe ten minutes."

Angie went weak at the knees. The doctor caught her by the arm and led her to a chair beside Jackie's bed. Angie sat there, stunned. Who should she call? She couldn't even think let alone pick up the phone and talk to anyone. What would she say? Their parents were visiting friends in Boston. It would take them hours to arrive. Angie's boyfriend was at home with the kids. Aunt's? Uncles? Who?

Movement in the bed pulled her out of her thoughts. Her sister was moving her head and opening her eyes. Angie jumped up to be in her sister's view.

"Hey Jackie, it's me, Angie," she said as she touched her arm gently. "You're gonna be alright."

"Gigi?" Jackie replied. It was a nickname only

*the two of them shared. "I love you. I'm glad
you're here. I'm sorry. I have to go soon."*

"I know. The doc said ten minutes."

*"Not here, Gigi. Over there. To the other side."
Jackie whispered between gasps.*

*"No, NO," Angie pleaded. "Not yet, it can't be
now, IT CAN'T BE NOW!"*

*"It is now, Gigi. And it's okay. Everything is
okay."*

*"No, it's not!" Angie insisted through brimming
tears. "I need you Jackie. I need you to see my
kids grow up and help me plan their weddings and
…and… and everything else."*

"I'll be there, Gigi. I promise. I love you."

"I love you too, Jackie. Please don't go."

*Jackie took one last breath and then her spirit
was gone. Suddenly, all hell broke loose as
buzzers and bells started going off. Immediately
medical staff came rushing in.*

*A nurse grabbed Angie by the arm. "Please
wait outside."*

*Angie listened to the conversation from just
outside the door. Suddenly things got quiet. Then
a quiet voice toned, "Time of death, 8:32 p.m."
The medical staff hurried out of the room quietly,
avoiding eye contact. The last one out was the
doctor. "I'm sorry Ms. Delgato. Your sister is
gone. You can sit with her as long as you like."*

*Angie wandered back into the room, shocked.
"I can stay as long as I want," she whispered to
herself. "How long is that exactly? Never. I never
want to leave. If I leave, I make this moment real
and it just can't be." Angie sat absolutely frozen for
some unknown amount of time. Then she heard a
quiet bell sound and recognized it as a text alert
from a phone. But not hers. She looked around
and saw Jackie's purse. The medics must have*

brought it in. Instinctively she got up and retrieved the phone. She pushed the button to read the text and saw the message from Jackie's boyfriend. The screen lit up the message like a beacon.

WTF BITCH! how long
does it take a moron like
you to get a case of beer

Angie was stunned, then horrified. A cool calm rage filled every cell in her being. She scrolled down to see the previous messages. What she read shattered the remaining pieces of her heart as she realized Jackie's last communication was a vicious stream of texts from Jerry. Picking up her own phone, she dialed the phone number from the card the officer gave her earlier. He was in the waiting area finishing his paperwork when his phone rang.

He entered the room quietly and respectfully, looking at what remained of Jackie, lying in the hospital bed. Angie remembered her rage from earlier. Apparently the officer hadn't taken it personally and she was grateful now for his calm presence.

"I'm sorry for your loss, Ms. Delgato. How can I help you?"

"I want you to charge this man with murder," she said as she handed him the phone.

* * *

Then, slowly, Angie's vision began to dissolve. She was becoming aware of being back in the shop. She put one hand on the counter for stability and looked around to see if anyone was watching. The other hand still held the new cell phone. She was just catching her breath when it dinged, indicating a message just arrived. She

forced herself to take one big gulp of air and hit the
button that would reveal the message.

Hi Gigi
I love you and I am with you always.
Please move on and enjoy your life. Take
every opportunity at happiness and fun.
Don't miss a thing. I am standing beside you.
You must embrace the future, technology and
all, because it is the world of your children
and you must be there for them.
I will be here waiting for you when it
is your time to come. That won't be for many
many years yet, but time is different over
here and I won't mind the wait.
I love you,
Jackie

At that moment, Marybeth rounded the corner from
the back and stopped short as she saw Angie, standing
frozen with the cell phone in her hand, her face ashen
white and streaked with tears. 'Oh, shit" came quietly
out of Marybeth's mouth. She immediately kicked
herself for not staying around or warning Angie that
weird things had been happening. "Oh, God, Angie.
Come here and sit down." Marybeth took her by the
arm and led her to a sofa that was for sale in the shop.
They sat side by side as Angie sobbed. Marybeth had
no idea what was going on or what to do now.

When the silence finally broke, it was Angie who
asked, "What the hell just happened to me?"

"Well" Marybeth began, "I'm guessing you just
had a vision?" She tried to sound nonchalant.

"And why would you guess that?" There was an
edge of anger in Angie's voice.

Marybeth proceeded with caution. "Because," she started out slowly, "it's been happening to me and a few other people."

"What?" Angie's voice still sounded edgy.

"I'm sorry, Angie." Marybeth started picking up the pace. "It's, ah, been an odd couple of weeks. Strange things have been happening that I don't totally understand like images and memories coming into my head. I haven't said anything because I didn't want you to think I was crazy." She tried to sound calm to ease Angie's distress (and her own).

Slower now, Marybeth prompted, "Tell me what just happened."

Angie's edge eased as she told Marybeth about her vision and described it as being transported back in time. Marybeth just nodded her head in understanding. Angie told the story of her sister and how helpless she was to stop the violence.

"In the end, Jerry never did get charged with murder. However, when the police showed up to investigate, they had probable cause to search the property. It seems there were several illegal fire arms and large amounts of heroin in the spare room." Angie was smiling in satisfaction. "It added up to fifteen to twenty years in federal prison. Much more than a manslaughter charge would have gotten him." Angie hesitated a moment at the thought. "But the truth is, he murdered my sister. And her story will never be told. There's no justice for her, no one will be held accountable."

Angie shifted her posture, finding her anger again.

"Did you know that every nine seconds a woman in this country is assaulted, EVERY NINE SECONDS, and three women every day are murdered by a partner?

Why are we not enraged!" She took a calming breath. "Sorry, I get on my soap box every once in a while about this stuff. No one honors my sister or the others who have fallen victim to the war against women."

Marybeth thought of the women at the shelter. She knew Angie was right. They were silent unseen victims.

"I know, Angie. I see it every time I go to the shelter. And there's never enough assistance to go around. Even their abusers seem to have more rights than they do!" Marybeth paused, realizing she was also getting soap-boxy herself.

"Oh, I guess I can get there too," she smiled. They both let out an awkward laugh, breaking the intensity of the moment. "I need a cup of coffee. How 'bout you?"

"I wouldn't turn it down," Angie replied as she took in a deep breath.

"I'll be right back."

When she returned from the cafe across the street, business went along as usual, in an unusual sort of way. Neither one attempted to open up more of the morning's conversation, opting for the comfort of the usual routine, both quietly reflecting on recent events.

Chapter 17

Marybeth took the morning off to see her mother. She was becoming more curious about the stories of her life and her family. This morning, between classes, was the only time her mother could squeeze her in, which irritated Marybeth more than slightly. It wasn't the kind of meeting she had hoped for but she took it, figuring that a time limited conversation might be best after all.

She was beginning to realize that she *was* still angry at them. Angry at her father for being so difficult and at her mother for not figuring out how to make it work. Whatever happened to staying together for the children? She remembered what Grams said just a week ago about mom trying to prove something. The photo from the yard sale seemed to be taking her to her own mother by way of Grams. Was she up for another heated conversation with Mom? It didn't matter. The stage had been set.

Arriving at the Campus Care before her mom, she found a table in the far corner. She was considering how to open the conversation when her mom approached carrying a planner and a cup of coffee. "Hi Sweetie," she said leaning over to give Marybeth a peck on the cheek before sitting down. "How are you?"

"Great Mom. How are you?"

"I talked to Grams last week. She said you were asking

lots of questions."

"Really, Mom? Not even any small talk?"

"We don't have time."

"I'm just getting curious about our family, that's all," she lied.

Her mother knew it was a lie. "I have another class in forty-five minutes, so, what would you like to know?" Mom eased up a little and took on a more inviting tone.

"Why did you divorce Dad?" Marybeth blurted out.

"How much time do you have?" Mom replied with a grin.

"Seriously, Mom."

"Okay, okay." Her mom put her hands up in surrender. She took a long deep breath that seemed to carry her back to a time far away. "It was a long time ago, Marybeth, and I can only tell it like I remember it. If you are going to ask your father for corroboration, his story might be different." Mom sounded irritated.

"I'm just trying to understand," Marybeth hoped this conversation would go better than previous ones.

"I don't see why it's so hard to understand, especially after your own marriage failed."

Anger shot up Marybeth's spine. "Thank you for your assessment of my marriage."

"Isn't that what you are about to do to me?" Mom shot back.

Marybeth paused long enough to realize that her mother was right, damn it.

Mom took advantage of the pause to say calmly "So, do you want to know or not?"

"I want to know." Marybeth was fighting to stifle her anger.

"It's taken me a long time to figure it out myself, Marybeth. You know, things are complicated. I was eighteen when I got married and twenty-six when I got divorced. You can't understand what my life was like without understanding the times I grew up in." Mom paused and took another deep breath as if she were inhaling the past into her body.

"Even if you weren't directly involved in the counterculture wave of the '60s, you couldn't help but be effected by it. I was young and idealistic, marching on Washington before I graduated from high school. I felt like Grams didn't understand anything, but now I think maybe I underestimated her." Marybeth noticed a slight pain cross her mother's face at this admission.

"Anyway, I met your father on one of those marches in 1970 when I was seventeen. He was twenty."

"Grams said you were handcuffed to the gate at Arlington National Cemetery and arrested together," Marybeth interrupted, suppressing a grin.

"Well, Grams sometimes confuses the facts for the sake of the story. We weren't the ones handcuffed and arrested. We were there in more of a support capacity." They both looked at each other for a long second before they burst out laughing. It instantly eased the tension.

"He'd already been to Vietnam and back by then and was actively protesting the war. I was too naive at the time to understand that he was also a little too heavy into drugs and alcohol." Mom noticed a wince from Marybeth at this information. "Yeah, well, you don't know it all, do you?"

Mom went on to talk about the turmoil of the times. Women's Liberation was changing the social rules - that and the birth control pill. Women were burning bras. Men were burning draft cards. The war was starting to fall out of favor. And still, young men continued to be sucked up into the military machine and spit out later. A lot of them came back with serious injuries, some visible, some not.

"When I met Dad, he seemed to have it together. He was handsome, articulate and excited to be involved in social change. He was going to force Washington to get off their asses and get out of Vietnam." Mom raised a fist in the air, smiling at the memories. "He had a bad boy charm and devil-may-care attitude." Marybeth saw the same twinkle in her mother's eye that she'd seen in Grams' a few day earlier. She wondered if her eyes would ever twinkle when she thought of Eric?

"We continued to meet up at events and then at coffee shops while I was in high school. When I got the scholarship to West Chester University, he decided to use his GI bill and started the same year. We were pretty idealistic back then, planning on taking the world by storm. Ha." Mom stopped to shake her head at the memory.

"It wasn't long before we were talking about getting married even though it wasn't very popular at the time. And then I got pregnant," Mom said, leaving this information hanging in the air. Even though Marybeth did the math years ago, Mom explained it by saying Marybeth was premature.

"What! You told me I was an early baby!" Marybeth cried foul.

"Yeah, well, it wasn't exactly a bragging point, especially back then." Mom collected her thoughts and went on. "There was no Roe v. Wade at the time. The right to a safe legal abortion didn't hit the books until 1973. Not that I would have seriously considered it.

Once we got over the shock, we were ecstatic. It was a time when *free love* was all the rage and the counterculture was challenging every aspect of life, including the composition of families."

Marybeth was shocked. "What did Grams say?" she asked, breathless.

"Grams about had a cow," mom chuckled. "She mentioned giving the baby up for adoption but we weren't having anything to do with that."

Marybeth allowed her brain to take a brief detour into her fantasy of adopting a baby in the 70s, noticing the irony that she might have been one of those babies.

Mom continued, "Grams raised a headstrong daughter and she knew there was no changing my mind, so she did her best to be excited for us. Gramps, on the other hand, did not. I think the day I got married was the most miserable day of his life," she said with a little sadness. "Maybe he knew first hand about the damages of war. Maybe he knew the toll it would take on our marriage. I don't know. He never said. He was the type that just shut down behind walls that were ten feet thick. Gramps suffered through the wedding, which took place in a public park."

"Wait a minute," Marybeth interrupted. "I thought you got married at the courthouse?"

"Well," mom paused. "Technically, it was the park *in front* of the courthouse."

"Oh my God! My entire life has been a lie."

"Stop being so dramatic. We just stretched the truth a little bit. What are you supposed to tell young children when they start asking questions?" Mom shrugged her shoulders. "We did the best we could is all I can say."

"Okay, so tell me about this wedding in the park."

"I'll just say it involved lots of tie-dye and love beads."

"Oh my god! Really?" Marybeth was stunned. "Please say it didn't include jeans and T-shirts."

Ignoring the question with a wave of the hand, Mom continued, "Grams and Gramps were completely horrified by the whole event. Dad's parents didn't show up at all. His relationship with them was already on the rocks. The pregnancy and wedding were more than they could handle. They came around a little when you were born, showing up at the hospital and meeting Gram and Gramps for the first time."

"I can't believe you never told me this."

"This is the first time you've ever pushed for the details."

"That's why we never saw much of Dad's parents."

"Dad's mom held a certain contempt for me. I'm sure she thought I trapped her son into marriage though she never said it out loud. Not to me at least. They would eventually become more involved but they never completely accepted things."

"That must have been hard on Dad."

"It wasn't easy. That, and the stress of having a baby, unmarried, and marginally employed, wore him down. It worried me too. I'm not going to lie. I went from thinking I knew everything to the slow realization that I didn't know that much at all. While I was having my own *spiritual awakening* Dad was going downhill fast."

"I had no idea." Marybeth was shocked by all this news.

"Not surprising see as you weren't born yet. At first we shunned the convention of a baby shower as being too old fashioned. Then we realized there was no way we were going get what we needed. Grams managed to scare up a few family and friends. I added a few names to the list and we managed to get the basic stuff like a crib and car seat. I'll admit, I was starting to get a little scared. I was nineteen remember, and clueless. Suddenly the independence I was demanding didn't look like such a good idea. I was hoping our friends would help out but when I looked around, all I saw was a bunch of hippies with no money and no common sense saying 'Oh, great that your having a baby. Very cool.' "

Mom's head was swaying side to side as if she were high. Marybeth couldn't help but let out a laugh.

"Yeah, real funny," Mom smiled. "Then there were the radical Women's Libbers hoping it was a girl so they could 'bring her up right'." Mom pounded a fist on the table, jostling the silverware.

Grabbing things quickly to quell the noise, they both looked around to see if they'd attracted any attention. Realizing no one cared, then broke into giggles.

"Oh, my God. It's a wonder we survived at all." Marybeth was still smiling as she shook her head.

"Anyway," Mom got a little more serious, "to her credit, Grams stepped in whether I liked it or not. I wouldn't give her the satisfaction of hearing it back then, but her help meant everything to me."

"It's not too late to tell her."

"No, I suppose it's not," Mom reflected for a moment before she went on. "As soon as you were born, your dad got clean. He still had his..."

"Wait. Wait. Wait." Marybeth interrupted. "What do you mean, 'got clean'?"

"What it usually means. He stopped using drugs

and alcohol, went to treatment, and got an AA sponsor."

"Are you kidding?"

"No."

"Does he still have one?"

"You'll have to ask him. I am no longer your father's keeper." The tone in Mom's voice shut the topic down with finality.

According to Mom they both continued with their education programs but she became the primary care taker for the baby.

"So much for women's lib," Mom said rolling her eyes. "All it got me was full-time school *and* a full-time family. Next thing I know, I'm pregnant again." Mom paused to take a breath.

"Well, Mom. It's not like you didn't know how that stuff happens," Marybeth challenged.

"Yes, well, sometimes things just happen no matter what your plans are. Anyway, it turned out great in the end and we have your lovely sister. We were both a little more mature by then and finishing school. Your father still left most of the parenting to me and I counted on Grams more and more. She was a trouper, putting up with my self-righteous attitudes about everything from diaper rash to discipline. As naive as I was, I knew by the time your sister was born that the marriage wasn't going well."

Marybeth sat, speechless, as she took in this information that Mom seemed to be downloading. She had no idea that things were that rough for her family when she was a baby. She took a moment to consider this new ever-changing picture of her life.

Mom continued, "My ongoing mantra became 'It will get better when. . .'" Marybeth caught her breath for an instant as her own words were coming out of her mother's mouth. Maybe she was more like her mother than she let herself believe.

"But *when* always came and went. Graduation and meaningful employment didn't improved things much. Dad became distant and irritable, jumpy even. We would argue and bicker about the smallest of things. Life began to look a lot like Grams and Gramps and I wasn't willing to settle for that like my mother did."

There it was, just as Grams suspected. "So you divorced Dad? Just like that? To prove something to Grams?" Marybeth's tone was accusatory.

"No, not 'just like that'! Did you divorce Eric 'just like that'?"

"That was different!"

"Yes, of course it was," her mother rolled her eyes. "No one divorces 'just like that.' It's a huge decision, even bigger than getting married in the first place and I agonized over it. But I'd already tried everything else I could think of to make it work. I sure as hell wasn't going to work harder than Dad, and it seemed like he wasn't working very hard at all." Mom looked down at her coffee in reflection. "I did the best I could, Marybeth."

Suddenly Marybeth felt like a heel, berating her mother for something that happened thirty years ago. What an ass she was being. "I'm sorry, Mom. I guess I'm still a little angry."

"Ya think? Look, you and your sister turned out to be beautiful, smart, capable women despite the momentary upheaval."

Mom was right. When was Marybeth going to let everyone off the hook? In another thirty years?

"We even tried counseling, which was not that popular back then."

"I didn't know you went to counseling."

"You were eight, Marybeth. What were we supposed to tell you?" Mom replied. "Marybeth, sweetie, I did everything I could think of to make things better but Dad was just stuck in his funk. I watched my mother live with my father's misery and I vowed I would never live like that. It wasn't until we got divorced that he finally got help."

"What do you mean?" asked Marybeth surprised.

"Well, that's Dad's story to tell honey. I imagine you'll be talking to him, too."

"That's my plan."

Mom looked at her watch. "I have to head back to class. I'll see you soon." She kissed Marybeth on the cheek and left. Marybeth sat there for a while absorbing the information. When she looked up at the clock, it was 12:45. Startled at the time, she quickly headed to her shop to open for the afternoon. As she drove away, she replayed the morning's conversation, adding the newest pieces to her puzzle. She was beginning to see a picture that was quite a bit different than she originally thought. What would it look like after she talked with Dad?

Chapter 18

It was Wednesday morning and Marybeth was in the garage when she heard the phone ring. It was Josh. He called almost every day to talk about the sale and chit chat for a few minutes. She had to admit, she was starting to look forward to his calls.

"Hey MB. It's Josh."

"I know. I have caller ID."

"Yeah, right." he hesitated, "Listen, I was wondering if you wanted to go out to dinner tonight."

"What for?" she asked, naively thinking it had something to do with the estate sale.

"To eat?"

"I can eat at home, thanks."

Josh paused. "Okay, how about I get a do-over?"

She noticed Josh was getting a little flustered. "A what?" she asked.

"A do-over. You know, how about if I start again."

"Okay."

"Hey, MB. How's it going?"

"Fine, Josh, thanks for asking."

"Would you like to go out to dinner with me tonight?"

"Like on a date or something?" she asked awkwardly.

"Yeah, like a date."

"Tonight?"

"Yeah, tonight, if you don't have anything planned."

"No, no plans. Where would we go?"

"I hadn't decided. I thought you might choose since you know the area better than I do."

"Okay. I have to tell you, though. I haven't been on a date in fifteen years."

"Seriously?"

"Yeah, seriously," she said a little defensively. "One year dating my husband, two years living together, ten years married, finishing off with two years divorced and disinterested. So no, I haven't been out on a date in a while."

"Okay then. How about breaking that streak?"

"So, let's say I do this. How does it work exactly? Like, do you pick me up? Are you paying?"

"I would be delighted to pick you up at your home if that feels okay to you. I will pay for all expenses for the evening."

"Do I have to get dressed up?"

"It depends on where you want to go. It's your choice."

Marybeth paused for a moment remembering many conversations with Regina about dating and that most men are just looking for sex so she added "And just so we are clear, we are not having sex for dessert."

Josh coughed as the chuckle got caught in his throat. "Understood. But I might want to kiss you goodnight."

"Maybe."

"Where would you like to go?"

Marybeth picked a family-owned restaurant one town over. She knew how people loved to talk and was hoping she would not be seen by anyone.

"What time can I pick you up."

"I'm an early bird. I'm not staying out all night."

"Understood."

"6:00."

"Where can I pick you up?"

Marybeth hesitated a moment then gave him the address.

"Okay," he said pausing for an awkward moment.

"Okay," Marybeth repeated.

"I'll see you tonight."

"I'll see you tonight," she agreed, and hung up.

Her heart was racing and she was barely breathing. "Oh, my God, I have a date." She finally exhaled and fanned herself with her hand. Get a grip, she told herself. It's just a date. Annoyed with herself she said out loud, "Distract yourself. Do something else." She went back to what she was doing in the garage, using busy work to fight back the wave of nervous nausea that was creeping in. This strategy didn't help much so she went to Plan B and got some coffee. Fortunately, the morning pot was still warm. As she sat in the kitchen drinking her coffee, she thought about Josh and wondered if he was feeling equally out of sorts. She hoped he was.

Josh, on the other hand, went into full panic mode. Truth was, he hadn't been out on a date in ten years but he certainly wasn't going to say that! The only thing he could think to do was call his brother. He was grateful when Rick answered the phone. Josh small-talked his way through recent events regarding the estate when his brother finally asked, "So, why are you calling me, because this is not new information."

"I've met someone," Josh said. There was a

moment of hesitation on the other end of the phone. "She's the first interesting woman I've met since Jan."

Chapter 19

Marybeth obsessed about the evening plans for most of the morning and finally called her sister for support.

"Regina, I have a date tonight."

"Wow. Really?"

"Don't sound so surprised," Marybeth replied, feigning hurt feelings.

"Okay." Regina said, pausing to start over. "Wow, a date. I'm not surprised. You go out so often on dates, how did you ever fit another one in?" Regina's exaggerated sarcasm came with a little chuckle.

"It's not funny. It's freaking me out."

"Okay, okay. Don't worry." Regina stifled a giggle. "I'll grab a couple of sandwiches and come over for lunch."

"Okay. Thanks. Marybeth felt better already. Regina had much more experience at these things. Reggie spent most of her adult life dating, until she finally settled down with her current live-in boyfriend about a year ago.

"Wow," Regina said as she walked in the door and took one look at Marybeth. "You must really like this guy."

"I don't know if I really like this guy," Marybeth said defensively. "I don't even know how I would know if I did."

"Well, one indication is if you get suddenly stupid when you think of him." Regina looked at her and grinned.

"Okay, okay, I'm guilty…and suddenly stupid. So you have to help me out here."

They spent the lunch hour laughing and reviewing the do's and don't's of dating, which didn't seem to be much help.

Don't ask him about past girlfriends.

Don't talk about your ex.

Don't cuss.

Don't complain.

Marybeth finally asked about the do's.

"There really aren't that many do's" Reggie admitted. "Just be yourself and relax. Think of it as if you are interviewing him for the job of Boyfriend."

"Please don't say that word. It makes me nervous."

"Okay, companion, new best friend, business associate if you have to," Reggie countered. "Have a glass of wine if you want, but only one. That can help take the edge off." Marybeth knew she wouldn't be drinking alcohol. She couldn't imagine dimming her wits any more than they already were.

"And no sex," Reggie added almost as an afterthought.

"No shit," was Marybeth's instant reply. "I'm freaking out because he said he wants to kiss me goodnight. It's unlikely to go much further than that."

"Did he really say that? About kissing you goodnight?" Reggie asked.

"Yeah. After I told him I wasn't going to have sex with him."

Regina burst out laughing. "Okay, good to get that out of the way," she said as they moved into the bedroom to pick out clothes.

"What will we talk about. I hardly know him," Marybeth complained as she rummaged through her shirts.

"First dates, by definition, are with someone you hardly know," Regina said kiddingly. "You ask him questions and you talk about yourself."

"Oh, great. He'll be asleep before the entree," Marybeth sighed.

"Stop thinking like that," Regina said, suddenly serious. "You are a delightfully interesting person and he will be enchanted with you."

"I'm not sure I want that."

"Yeah. That's why you called me over to coach you and pick out your clothes, because you're not interested." Reggie chuckled.

They picked out a fitted knit top with a low neck line. Marybeth immediately threw an over-sized sweater over it.

"What are you doing!" Regina said horrified. "Take that off."

"I can't go out in just this! It's skin tight."

"That's the point. Hello? Looking attractive not frumpy is the goal."

Regina grabbed a long silk scarf while Marybeth reluctantly removed the sweater.

"There. Perfect," she concluded, draping it around her neck.

Marybeth stepped back to look in the full-length mirror. Black chinos and black pumps finished off the outfit and she had to admit, it looked a little spicy.

"Are you sure about this? It feels a little weird."

"You mean a little hot. You're just not used to looking attractive. I don't remember the last time you dressed for an evening out."

"Fifteen years, give or take."

"I believe it. So trust me on this. You look

fabulous."

As Regina's lunch hour was coming to a close, they quickly created a bail-out strategy. Regina would call thirty minutes into the date. If Marybeth picked up the phone, Regina would have some excuse why Marybeth had to leave abruptly. If Marybeth didn't pick up the phone, she was required to call Regina as soon as she got home. 'To make sure she was okay' was the excuse, but they both knew it was so Regina could pump her for the details. With one last bit of reassurance, Regina headed back to work. Marybeth changed back into everyday attire. Was it really frumpy? Maybe. She considered revamping her wardrobe as she headed to the shop to open for the afternoon.

Chapter 20

The shop was slow, giving Marybeth plenty of time to angst about the evening plans. She kept herself busy in between customers, answering emails and updating inventory. It occurred to her that she could Google Josh and see if she could find out more about him. She wondered if somehow that was cheating. She decided it was not. It was all public information after all. So she opened the search screen and typed in "Josh Anderson." Instantly, a page full of potentially interesting sites popped up. As she reviewed the list, she noticed that they were all articles and short stories he wrote covering many years and many topics. It seems Josh had an opinion on just about everything but most of the articles were about the environment and politics. As she scrolled down, a different kind of title caught her attention. *Leela's Lei*. Marybeth clicked through to the website. *Leela's Lei* was an environmentally conscious children's book, written in 2007 by Joshua Anderson and illustrated by Janet Morrison. The website included beautiful sample pages from a book written for young children ages three to six.

Marybeth reflected back on thirteen years of teaching. She had taught all of the elementary grades but she liked kindergarten the best of all. The undying curiosity and innocent questions of five-year-olds never ceased to bring her joy. The children delighted her at every turn. She wondered if she would ever return to teaching. If she did, maybe she would read Josh's book with them.

Just then a customer jolted her out of her search. Marybeth felt like she was caught doing something wrong.

"Can I help you?" she blurted out almost too loudly.

"Yes, I'm looking for items for a new mother," the woman said, pinging that old sadness in Marybeth's heart again. "This is an unexpected pregnancy and the new mom is a bit freaked out."

"I'm sorry to hear that. I'm afraid I don't have much but I can keep an eye out if you like and call you if I have anything," Marybeth offered. She hated to admit it but her curiosity was up.

"That would be very sweet. Why don't I check back with you in a couple of weeks," the woman suggested.

"Sure thing." As the door closed behind her, Marybeth looked up at the clock and noticed it was closing time, five o'clock. She fought back nervous jitters as she locked up and headed home to change. Her nerves only got worse as she was getting dressed. God, she thought, is this what it's going to be like for me every time I have a date? Maybe I'll just stay single. Maybe I'll get a friend with benefits. Isn't that what people are doing nowadays? No, that was essentially what Eric was doing and she knew it wasn't for her. She finally managed to stop the whirlwind in her head by remind herself that this was just dinner. Regina's words popped into her head, "suddenly stupid," and she laughed at herself.

Right on time, the doorbell rang. Marybeth had seen him drive up but wasn't sure what the etiquette was so she waited till he got to the door. She felt completely awkward and was beginning to get angry at herself for getting so caught up in this. Once again her sister's words rang like bells in her head and she smiled to herself.

"Hi," she said as she opened the door.

"Hi. Are you ready to go?" Josh asked.

"Yes," was all she could think of to say.

"Great. I have my car tonight. I drive my mother's car a couple times a week just to keep it going."

"Oh, really? Just to keep it going?" Marybeth chided.

"Okay, because it's fun too." Josh admitted with a boyish grin. "But tonight, I thought we'd trade muscle for style." And sure enough, parked in the driveway was a smokey gray Jaguar.

"Wow. You're not kidding. Very nice."

"I have the GPS set up to get us to the restaurant, but you might know a better way. So, feel free to be copilot."

Marybeth had never used a GPS around town. Why would she? But she was interested to see how well it did.

"I'll jump in if I feel the need," she said.

"Great." He opened the car door for her, then slid into the driver's seat and pulled out of the driveway.

"Turn left," a sexy female voice was saying as they approached the stop sign. Marybeth smiled, wondering if she could get one with an alluring male voice.

They drove for a while in silence letting Trixi (she silently named the GPS person) lead the way. Marybeth was starting to feel suddenly stupid again. Thinking of her sister, she laughed to herself and relaxed. "How are things with the estate going?" she asked which launched them into safe conversation for the remainder of the drive. They got to the restaurant with ease, Trixi being an efficient navigator, and were seated quickly.

It was a small family-owned place with tables for two by the windows and larger round tables for families in the center. There was a bar at the far end with half a dozen stools and two beer taps. It seemed to be used mostly by those waiting for a table.

As soon as they sat down, Josh noticed a good-looking older man approaching the table from behind Marybeth. When he reached her side, he reached down and took her hand. Kissing it gently, he said with a big smile, "Marybeth, what a nice surprise to see you here. I hope we are still on for Sunday."

Marybeth, caught off guard, glanced over at Josh who had gone pale. She looked up at her admirer, smiled and said "Yes, Dad. Right after you get home from church." She heard Josh exhale.

"Dad, this is Josh. He's a business associate."

Dad reached out to shake hands as Josh stood up to do the same. "Hi. I'm Sean" he said smiling.

"Nice to meet you," Josh managed.

Sean was waving with his hand at Josh, "Sit down, sit down." As Josh sat back down, Marybeth was looking around "Are you with Sue tonight?"

"Not tonight. I'm on my own. I didn't feel like cooking so I came by for some takeout. A business associate, eh?" he continued, looking from one to the other.

"I'll explain on Sunday, Dad. See you then," she added before the conversation could go any further.

"Ah, yes," he responded, taking the hint. "It was nice to meet you Josh."

"Likewise," Josh replied.

As she watched her dad walk away, she had to admit that he was quite a handsome man at sixty-one. He kept himself in good shape and attended to his health, as the fifteen bottles of supplements in his cabinet would attest. The result was a slender, graceful man with a charming smile. Suddenly she saw the man her mother fell in love with.

"So, Sunday will be the follow-up conversation to the one with your mother?" Josh asked. Marybeth had been sharing her new family stories with Josh in an effort to gain some perspective.

"Yeah, I can hardly wait," she rolled her eyes.

They took a minute to order dinner and then eased into safe conversation about Josh's mother and her estate. Josh talked about all the legal threads that his brother was attending to. Unfortunately most things still had to pass through the Pennsylvania courts, so he ended up running papers here and there anyway. Marybeth found it all interesting, knowing that sooner or later she would do the same for her parents.

Then Josh changed the subject and it was Marybeth's turn to share. "So, how long have you owned the store?" Josh asked.

"Just over a year. I ran it by myself for the first six months, then picked up Angie to work the weekends. It's been fun but I never intended it to be more than a temporary thing. I always thought I would go back to teaching when the dust settled."

"And what dust would that be?"

"That would be divorce. It was a dusty one."

"Sorry to hear that. So before that you were teaching?"

"I was a kindergarten teacher for eight years when my marriage fell apart. At the time, I didn't have the energy to return to school but I needed income and things just evolved."

"So, you never had children?" Josh asked innocently.

Marybeth winced internally at the question. Most people knew her situation and avoided the topic all together. She pushed herself to have the conversation. "We tried," she managed to reply. "It wasn't in the cards for us I guess." She realized the reference to tarot cards as soon as she said it. How many times had she used the phrase without thinking about it. She suddenly felt awkward, exposed even. Fortunately, the waiter arrived with dinner placing a plate of Shrimp Scampi in front of Josh and Pork Chop with Rice in front of Marybeth, before darting off to another table.

They looked at each other a minute then laughed as they switched plates to the rightful owners. Josh picked up the conversation where they left off.

"My mom had a hard time having kids. She had a few miscarriages along the way. She considered my brother and me her miracle babies. For a long time I felt like I had to do something extraordinary with my life because of it. It can be pretty daunting when I think about it. My parents would say they didn't care what I did as long as I'm happy. Still., sometimes I think I should do more or be more. "

"Yes," she agreed. "That whole idea of when is it enough...whatever. Enough time, enough money, enough pain. When is it okay to quit! It still kicks my . ." She suddenly remembered what Reggie said about cursing. "butt," she finished.

Josh laughed at her self-censoring.

"Yes, it does," he agreed.

There was a moment of silence and Marybeth

wondered about the time, energy and money she and Eric had spent trying to conceive and if it would have been better spent in almost any other way. She often got angry at herself, thinking of her efforts as foolish attempts to override fate. This was usually the point where she got angry with God.

"So," Marybeth began, "Explain to me what it means to see auras," effectively changing the subject.

"Well, it's not quite as mysterious as it seems. Ever since I can remember, I saw a shadow around people. I never knew what they were until I was older. My mom told a great story about it. I don't remember it but according to her, after spending the afternoon with the neighbor boy, I asked my mother why my friend was green. My mother, trying to figure out what exactly I was asking, asked what color he usually was. I said he's usually yellow. She asked me what color my brother was. I said he changes a lot but mostly red. She asked about herself and I told her she was white. Keep in mind that my mom was already wandering into the metaphysical world. She knew that she had a way of knowing things that other people didn't know."

Josh hesitated a moment in his story waiting to see if Marybeth was blowing him off like most people. When she stayed silent, he offered her an out.

"Are you sure you want to hear this? It gets a little bizarre for most people."

"I'm not most people," she said, sounding harsher than she wanted to. She flashed him a smile, trying to take the edge off it. "Let's just say I'm becoming intimately familiar with the bizarre." With a hand gesture, she bade him continue.

Josh nodded, silently acknowledging the statement and then went on. "My mom started asking around and found someone who had a similar vision. She asked him all kinds of questions until she was sure that it wasn't harmful to me in any way. She never discouraged me or told me to keep it a secret but it wasn't long before I realized that other people didn't see the colors I saw." Josh looked down as if recalling some moment in time.

"What happened?" Marybeth prompted.

"There was a time at school. I was fifteen. I was hanging out in the school courtyard before the first bell. I was with a few of my buddies and we were keeping an eye on a group of girls nearby," he smiled at the adolescent memory.

"I'll bet you were. And I'll bet they were keeping an eye on you too."

"I'm sure they were," he nodded with a smile. "Anyway, suddenly, one of the girl's colors went really dark really fast. I freaked out and ran over to her asking if she was okay. She looked at me strangely and said yes, of course she was okay and what was wrong with me. I got all flustered, mumbled some apology, and turned back to my friends. A moment later, she collapsed. It ended up being juvenile diabetes, but we didn't know that for a couple of weeks. In the meantime I quickly became the school freak and only a few close friends would talk to me."

"Ooohhh. That sounds horrible."

"It was a rough year, and a hard lesson." He took a deep breath seeming to exhale the memory. "Needless to say, I didn't mention it much after that. I learned to ignore it, looking at it as just the way someone looked, like a haircut or something they were wearing that day."

"So, what do the auras mean?"

"I don't really know. I looked into it a little as an

adult but by that time it was just the way I saw the world. Nothing more."

"Then why did you bring it up at the shop that day we met?"

"Because your aura was doing strange things."

"Are you saying I'm strange?" she asked smiling.

"I would never say that." He smiled back.

"Because, Mr Anderson, if we were in a Strangeness Contest you would get the top Strangest of the Strange Award."

"And, Ms. Collette, I would graciously accept the Strangest of the Strange Award. This might come as a surprise to you, but I've received it quite often in my life."

"I'm not surprised at all."

They were both glad for a silly break in a conversation that had turned a little too serious perhaps. They continued with a light banter back and forth, laughing and appreciating the humor. Josh turned the conversation around again.

"So, you get visions," he said.

Marybeth almost choked on her food. "I don't get visions," she shot back, immediately defensive.

"Okay," Josh paused, "What do you call it then, when you 'remember things that you have forgotten that you knew'?" he asked, using her own words. She now understood the saying 'Make sure your words are sweet. You may have to eat them later.' Just then, her phone rang.

"Oh my God. I'm sorry. I forgot to turn it off. Let me just do that now." She fumbled in her purse for the phone. She looked at the caller. It was Regina. She had completely forgotten. For a brief moment she considered taking the call, then turned the phone off and put it back in her purse.

"Now, where were we?" She feigned memory loss in hopes of changing the subject.

"You were about to tell me about the visions you don't have."

"Oh. Right." Somewhat reluctantly, somewhat gratefully, Marybeth shared pieces of the yard sale story and how it seemed to have ignited this new experience of visions. "I picked up this doll and got a vision of the old woman as a child who saw her sister killed in a car accident. Then, next thing I know, I'm standing on the lawn again, almost like nothing happened, except it did. When I looked over at the old woman, she was just sitting there, looking at me."

Marybeth shook her head and shrugged her shoulders as if confused.

"Sounds a little weird," Josh acknowledged.

"A *little*?" The story started spilling out of her mouth as if dying to be told. "Then she asked me if I had a sister and it made me think about the rift between me and Regina. Then, out of nowhere, Reggie calls. She came over, picked up the doll and had her own vision. It's all been hard for me wrap my brain around. Add to that, all this family stuff and, well, sometimes I think I'm just going crazy."

She paused to take a breath and reflect over all the events of the past few weeks. The visions were causing her to question reality, yes, but all the knew information from her family was shaking her to the core. She constantly wondered what long-held *truth* would be the next to go.

Josh was reassuring her of her sanity as dessert arrived, a Double Chocolate Ice Cream Brownie with two spoons.

"After you," He indicated she take the first spoonful with an exaggerated wave of his hand.

"Such a gentleman," she replied as she carved off a corner.

"Well," he went on, "for what's it's worth, I don't think you're crazy at all. Just unusual."

"Oh, that's so much better," she kidded.

The banter turned lighthearted as they finished off dessert. After which, Josh graciously payed the bill and they headed out the door.

They were pulling into her driveway when Marybeth started to get more nervous about the date. Oh, God, now what? She was thinking.

Without saying a word, Josh got out and walked around to open her door. He helped her out, which at this moment she was grateful for, as her knees were weak. Taking her hand, he walked her to the door. She knew her hand was trembling and she was pissed about it.

"Well," he said as they got to the door. He turned her to face him.

"Yeah," was all she could muster as she turned to the door in hopes of a quick escape. "Thanks for dinner."

"Not so fast," Josh responded, placing his hand on her arm and turning her gently back to face him. "We still have a kiss to finish off the evening."

"We do?" There was a nervous tremor in her voice.

"Yes, we do," he replied. "It is customary that dates end in a kiss. It's sort of like the hot fudge on a Sunday. You *could* skip it but it wouldn't really be a Sunday." Before Marybeth could dodge him again, he took her face gently in both hands, tipped it up to his own, and gently kissed her lips. It was a simple kiss that lingered just long enough to awaken a longing in Marybeth that she thought died years ago. She felt immediately vulnerable, as the ice cap on her heart cracked with an almost tangible bang inside her chest. Josh was still holding her face ever so gently when Marybeth opened her eyes. "Thanks, for the date," she said quietly.

"My pleasure," Josh replied, playing with her hair for a moment before stepping away from her. "I hope to do it again."

"Could happen," she replied as she opened her door. "Good night."

"Good night," he said as he turned to go.

She watched him walk to his car from the front window. When he was gone, she leaned herself against the wall by the door as tears filled her eyes. Her internal global warming was releasing all the grief of her marriage and divorce. She hadn't realized it till now but the ice cap had held the pain, safely contained, for years. She sobbed quietly as she slid down the wall she was leaning against. She wondered if she was up for this. She was letting the next wave of emotions subside when the phone rang from inside her purse. It was Regina. She knew she had to answer it. She picked up the phone, still sobbing. Regina, hearing the tears in her sister's voice, went into panic mode.

"Marybeth, oh my God, what happened? Are you alright? Where are you? Are you at home?"

"Yes," Marybeth managed to answer the last question first and was about to address the others when Regina interrupted

"I'll be right over." Click. The phone went dead.

"Oh great," she sighed. "I have thirty seconds to get myself together." Okay, she told herself. Make some tea. She allowed herself one more sob and a deep breath before she headed to the kitchen to put on a pot of water. She enjoyed herbal tea in the evening and realized now that it would help calm her nerves. Before she could even get the teas out of the cupboard, Reggie was blasting through the front door.

"Marybeth, Marybeth, where are you?" she called frantically.

"I'm in here," she called from the kitchen.

Reggie zoomed around the corner and grabbed her sister in a huge bear hug then held her sister out at arm's length and inspected her front and back for signs of foul play, the whole time repeating "Are you alright? What happened? Are you alright?" The only thing she could identify were puffy red eyes.

Marybeth felt bad that she upset her sister, but she couldn't help smiling at the overreaction. "Yes, dear, I'm fine. Really. Stop the panicking."

"My sister is sobbing on the phone after her first date in years with a complete stranger. What am I supposed to do?" she asked crossly.

Marybeth apologized and reassured Regina that she was okay, just a little emotional.

"How did the date go?" Regina's panic had subsided to concern.

"He was a perfect gentleman the entire time. He gave me a very sweet kiss at the door and then went home."

"Okay, I'm confused now," Regina said as she calmed herself down.

At that moment the tea kettle whistled. Marybeth poured them both some Calm Evenings tea and they sat at the kitchen table.

Marybeth explained, "I guess I'm just a little overwhelmed emotionally. I've been avoiding things for years, just sucking it up and moving on. But this whole thing with Josh has me a bit rattled."

"A bit?"

"Well, apparently it wasn't wrapped up as tightly as I thought and it appears the flood gates are seriously leaking."

The truth was that guilt and self-doubt had plagued her for years. She was unable to solve the problems in her marriage and unable to have a family. Things other people seemed to be doing with ease. What was she doing wrong? Or what was wrong with her? Maybe she wasn't as smart as she thought she was. Maybe she was defective in some way, unlovable, and should avoid relationships altogether?

Regina tried to be supportive. She's been single for years waiting for the right guy to come along.

"Now I understand that the right person today might not be the right person tomorrow. Things change. If the person I'm with can't or won't grow with me, then I know I can enjoy it while it lasts, be grateful and move on. Look, Marybeth, I know you did everything you could to save your marriage. If Eric wasn't willing to grow with you then he was holding you back."

"Maybe. But what if I just didn't wait long enough? What if the next time would have been the real change? What if..."

"Stop. You could not have single-handedly saved your marriage. If Eric wasn't on board, it wouldn't have mattered how long you stayed or what you said. It's time to let yourself off the hook and move on. Josh might not be the next great love of your life, but he's good company for now...and nice to look at, too." Regina added, trying to lighten the mood.

"Maybe, Reggie." She flashed a week smile. "I

don't know if I can look at things that way, but maybe it's a place to start."

"That's the spirit." She raised her coffee mug in a toast. "Now, I've been dying to know, how did things go with Mom?"

The conversation shifted to recent conversations with Grams and Mom as she filled Reggie in on the new dimensions that her life's picture was taking on. Regina listened intently adding the occasional "Really?" and "She really said that?" and "I never knew that." The conversation went long into the night as they both pieced together information and added their own perspective to it. In many ways it was an enlightening and healing conversation. They were both exhausted when it was over.

"Maybe you can drag your tired ass into work any time you want tomorrow, but I have to be at work at 8:45. And you have kept me up till 1:30," Regina kidded. She and Marybeth talked before about the stresses of each of their jobs and she knew Marybeth felt a lot of pressure to make the business work.

"Oh yes, being self-employed is like living in the lap of luxury, coming and going as I please" Marybeth replied. They hugged good night and Regina headed home.

Marybeth leaned against the closed door, thinking about how fast her life seemed to be changing. Despite Josh's earlier reassurance, once again she began to question her sanity. She made herself another cup of tea and headed to bed.

Chapter 21

Marybeth pulled into the driveway at her dad's house and sat for a moment to collect herself. She was excited and apprehensive. Talks hadn't gone any better with her dad over the years than they had with her mom. Too late to back out now without looking like a total coward. She steadied herself for an adversarial conversation.

The last few days had been quite an emotional ride and she felt fragile. The barrage of new information was chipping away at her longstanding defenses. Grams' bombshell took the first toll, weakening the system. Then, trying to integrate mom's conversation into her psyche over the past week had taken a few more chips out of it. Would Dad's conversation bring the whole thing down? If so, what then? Even though she had been on a mission to get answers, maybe she wasn't ready for them.

There was a part of her that didn't want to let go of the self-righteous anger that she had brandished about for years. It was starting to look like it was founded on her one-sided skewed perspective. With each new piece of information, she was forced to shift her thinking about who she thought she was.

"Helloooo," she called as she walked into the kitchen.

She could smell breakfast cooking which sparked her appetite, but she didn't see her dad anywhere. "Helllloooo," she called out again.

"I'm in the back," came a disembodied voice. "I'll be right out." And sure enough, Dad came around the corner an instant later carrying a white box and two photo albums. Marybeth immediately identified the white box as a wedding album.

"At the last minute, I remembered that I had these in the closet. I got them in the divorce, I guess you could say." He smiled sadly and shrugged his shoulders. He put them on the coffee table and headed into the kitchen to attend to the cooking.

"Mom told me you'd been asking questions, so I thought I'd jog my memory. And you know, a picture is worth a thousand words as the saying goes."

"Wow, great," Marybeth was saying. She had no idea there *were* pictures. As curious as she was, they could wait till after breakfast. Dad was a good cook and she'd been looking forward to it all week. Slow cooked bacon, fluffy scrambled eggs with a buttery cream sauce, and perfectly browned pancakes gave them time to catch up on current events. It was no time at all before the conversation got around to Marybeth's dinner date.

"A business associate? Really?" Dad said, tilting his head and raising an eyebrow.

"Yes, a business associate," Marybeth said a little irritated at the implication.

"Well, it's just that I haven't seen you that dressed up in years. Except for weddings and funerals of course. Do you think you'll have more *business* with him?"

"That's enough on that topic," Marybeth stated,

using her kindergarten teacher tone. Dad dutifully changed the subject.

"Sure. Okay. How about we talk about me?" he said half in jest as he cleared the dishes to the sink. "Refill your coffee (he knew she would anyway) and let's look at pictures."

They retreated to the living room, bringing their coffee with them and leaving the dishes for later.

"Tell me what you want to know," Dad said as they sat down, side by side on the couch, the albums on the table in front of them.

"Why did you and Mom get divorced?" she asked with a newfound directness.

"How much time do you have?" he asked causing Marybeth to reflect on how much alike he and Mom were even after all these years.

"Come on, it can't be that complicated."

"It's always that complicated, sweetie. Can you sum up your marriage and divorce in three sentences?"

"No, I suppose not," she relented. She wanted it to be simple though, if not for her then for her eight-year-old self who was asking.

"Those were crazy times," he began, again just like her mother. "And to tell you how it ended, I have to tell you how it started. I was just back from Vietnam. I was stationed for the last two months of my enlistment in Virginia, where I was on medical leave recovering from some injuries. To my surprise, I came home to a country that hated me, spit on me and called me 'baby killer.' They protested almost daily in front of the hospital."

"How long were you there?"

"Not long. Two and a half months to get a clean bill of health and an honorable discharge. The day I walked out the door, complete with my purple heart and combat medal, national guard troops opened fire on unarmed college students at Kent State. The news hit me in the gut. The entire country was in shock. The event was like throwing gasoline on the antiwar fire. I can't tell you how much that messed with my already messed-up head."

"Really?" She was instantly irritated. "You're playing the 'poor Vietnam vet not able to cope' card? But you did cope and you made out just fine. So, what does that have to do with anything?" Her old anger had reared up, loud and cutting.

"If you don't want to hear my story, then why are you here?" Dad was tired of her attitude already and wasn't pulling any punches.

His response pulled her up short. What *was* she doing here? "I don't know why I'm here," she shot back.

Dad waited silently for her apology.

"I'm sorry. I'm on a little bit of overload with all this family stuff."

"Is that an apology?"

"It's the best I can do at the moment."

Again, dad was silent.

"Alright. I'm sorry. I'll reign it in."

"Thank you." He continued, "It was only a little easier once I got back to Westfield, where things were toned down, but being home was hard in a different way. I started hearing from my folks about my high school friends that wouldn't be coming home, ever. I became wracked with guilt every time I saw family members of my fallen friends. I felt like there was an unasked question hanging in the air. 'Why my boy and not him?' It must have been hard for my parents too. Their friends had lost sons that were my age.

Eventually I moved out and distanced myself from everyone."

She found herself pulled into the story. "Where did you go?"

"A small town outside of DC. There was a company there hiring for warehouse workers."

"But you were injured."

"Nothing a few pain pills wouldn't take care of."

With growing awareness, Marybeth could see where this was going.

"I started getting active in the antiwar movement. I let my hair grow long and wore a bandanna around my head." Dad stopped to chuckle at the memory. "Those were the days."

"The '70s were known for their music not their fashion," Marybeth pointed out.

"You won't get an argument on that. Anyway, I joined a couple local activist groups to try to fit in. Even as I walked with them and waved their signs, I felt there were unasked questions that hung in the air. *What did he do over there? Is he a baby killer?* So I began to avoid lengthy conversations that might turn in that direction which distanced me more from other people."

"What *did* you do over there, Dad," Marybeth asked cautiously realizing that she knew almost nothing of her dad's life.

"Officially, my title was medic." Dad paused to let the memories filter in. "My assigned duty was to catalog the dead. 8,764 to be exact."

Marybeth raised her eyebrows and sucked in a breath.

He went on. "It's strange what sticks in your head. I kept a mental count of the soldiers I processed. Occasionally I would see the name of someone I used to know or I'd met just the other day passing through camp." He looked away for a moment, recalling some faraway time, then abruptly shook it off, returning to the living room and the present moment with his daughter.

"I met your mom in 1970 during an antiwar march to Valley Forge. She was young and beautiful and full of spirit, something that I had lost in Nam. She connected me back to the wonders of life and the daily miracles seen by the innocent and curious. She breathed life back into me. Problem was, I never started breathing on my own. I made mom responsible for my joy. Mom, and drugs. I gave up the drugs when you were born because I knew it was the right thing to do. That left me with just Mom who was busy taking care of a new baby."

"She said Grams helped out a lot."

"Yeah. That just made me feel worse. Like I couldn't take care of my own daughter. The truth was, I couldn't. Vietnam demons were creeping into my head. I started having nightmares, had a hard time sleeping. I was grumpy and irritable. I only left the house if I had to."

"I remember you checking the windows all the time."

"Yeah. I became hyper-concerned about safety, especially for you. They call it hyper-vigilance. When Regina was born, things got worse."

"Oh, my God. I had no idea."

"Of course not. You were a baby."

"Yeah, but..." She let the thought trail off.

"It was close to paranoia. It would consume me. I didn't feel safe anywhere. The doors at home had to be locked at all times. We lived on campus then and every little noise would put me on edge. Now I can imagine how difficult it was for Mom, but back then I just felt like she didn't understand me anymore and she didn't. I didn't even understand myself. I knew what I was thinking and doing was crazy but I couldn't stop. What I had was PTSD, Post Traumatic Stress Disorder, but it wouldn't be identified as a problem for vets for seven more years. The year after we were divorced, it became an official medical diagnosis."

"What did you do? I mean, you're fine. Right?"

"I got help. That's what I did. Counseling at the VA in Philly. I went there on Saturdays when I dropped you at Grams'."

"Wait. Wait." Marybeth was saying waving her hands. "You mean that when you dumped us at Grams, you were seeing a counselor?"

"Well, I didn't think of it as dumping you, but yes," Dad replied surprised.

"Oh my God, Dad. I thought you were seeing another woman! You always smelled like perfume when you got back!" She was getting angry now, realizing she had been misled by her own imagination. "It apparently never occurred to you to tell us! I've been mad at you for years for that!"

"Wow, sweetie, I had no idea. You're right. It *didn't* occur to me to tell you. You were so young. I didn't know how to explain it so I just left it alone. Maybe, if I were being honest, I was afraid you'd think I was crazy or be afraid of me. It never entered my mind that you would make up your own story about it. I'm so sorry."

Marybeth was sobbing now, tears of the rage and guilt rolling down her face. Dad put his arm around her and stroked her hair, seeing the little girl in her that had been betrayed so many years ago and feeling his own heart break. They sat like this for a while, Dad kissing her head, saying I'm sorry and crying his own tears.

She was desperately trying to tame the tornado that was going on in her head. How can this be? How can she have been so wrong all these years and yet so sure of herself. It had never occurred to her that she didn't have all the information or that there even *was* more information. She had held both her parents to task for years, but she had been especially angry with Dad.

"I'm so sorry, Dad," she managed to say between sobs.

"You don't have anything to be sorry for."

"Yes, I do. Don't let me off the hook so easy. I've been carrying a resentment against some imaginary woman and been angry at you for years when all you were doing was trying to get help. I'm such a jerk!"

"You're not a jerk. You were just a kid trying to make sense of things." Gently releasing her, Dad picked up their coffee cups and headed to the kitchen. He returned with fresh coffee and scones from the morning's breakfast. The man knew his daughter well. They ate, drank and apologized more until the air was clear and emotions had calmed down.

Marybeth finally changed the subject. "Okay, I'm ready for the next shock. Let's look at some of these wedding pictures," she said with a smile. "My curiosity is taking over. I can't wait to see it. I have imagined that you guys were barely dressed."

"To be honest with you, I don't remember it all that much myself so it will be a surprise for me too." They laughed together and Marybeth realized she has missed this for years.

As they opened the small box, Marybeth was

surprised to find what appeared to be a conventional wedding album inside. Conventional until you opened it, that is. As soon as she opened the cover, she was greeted with a sign of the times. A rolling paper was stuck to the inside cover of the album. On it was written "Our Wedding". She looked up at her dad who was trying not to grin.

"Yeah, well, ah. . ." he said as he reached up and turned the page.

Although it wasn't the psychedelic color explosion she had imagined, it was certainly unique. Her parents basically took all the fixings of a conventional wedding and blew it up with tie-die. Mom's traditional wedding dress, all white and fluffy, had been attacked by a pair of dress shears and accessorized with love beads. It was cut off just above the knees with a kerchief hem and a tie die sash around the waist. The tie-dyed veil served as the train, trailing about three feet behind her. Surprisingly, it was kind of cute and Marybeth made a mental note to grab the next wedding dress she found at a yard sale and see what she could do with it. Dad was adorned in a tie-die blazer and black pants. They both wore a wreath of flowers in their hair. All in all, it was far better than her mother described.

"Wow. That wasn't so bad," Marybeth commented as they closed the book.

"Yeah, well, you weren't there," Dad kidded.

"Do you think that you were really in love the day you got married? I mean, considering that eight years later you weren't any more."

"Of course we were in love. I never really considered that we fell *out* of love. I just think there were too many things in the way. At least for me. I don't know what story Mom told. She had a different perspective I'm sure. In a way, we're both right."

"Maybe you're both wrong?" she challenged him.

"No. I think time proved the story. We both went on to be much happier eventually. And we always agreed on things for you girls. Always." Dad took a deep breath. "And that's about all I have for you today. If you need to talk about anything else, call your sister." His smile was infectious. Marybeth was still chuckling on her way out to the car.

Chapter 22

It was the day before the Jack-o-Lantern Festival and scaffolding was going up all over the town common. Smaller units were already up along sidewalks and storefronts. Anyone and everyone was welcome to bring their carved or decorated pumpkins into town for the celebration. Last year over 8,000 Jack-o-Lanterns were lit up for two nights, beating the previous year's record of 6,783. They were hoping to set a new record this year. The largest pumpkin to be found would be carved and placed on the top of the forty foot scaffolding at one end of the common. Usually weighing in at over 400 pounds, it would be put in place on Friday afternoon using a crane donated by a local construction company. It would be ceremoniously lit by the town mayor at 6 p.m, signaling the start of the festival.

The festival energized the whole town. Many people came dressed up in wonderfully creative Halloween costumes. Certainly almost everyone would bring a pumpkin. The carvings ran the gamut from simple to dramatic to funny. There would be pumpkins as small as apples and as large as boulders. Last year a few people added color to their Jack-o-lanterns using glass candle holders inside. One die-hard romantic cut four pumpkins with the words 'Will you marry me?' It was always great fun.

The festival quickly built up a great reputation and

brought visitors in from Philadelphia and beyond, sending a burst of money into the local economy. In addition, it offered the local folks opportunities to meet their neighbors and make new friends through the many volunteer hours needed to pull it off. It was truly home-town family fun.

Marybeth was caught up in the excitement. She was sponsoring a set of scaffolding in front of her store along Main Street and she was planning on spending the evening with Josh carving a huge pumpkin for the top shelf. Josh had called her almost daily since their first, and only, date. Tonight might be considered date number two except they weren't actually going anywhere. Josh had been tasked with acquiring a pumpkin, big enough to stand out on her shelving and small enough to be lifted six feet up. He would arrive at the shop just after closing with pumpkin and carving tools.

Marybeth was outside the store cleaning up the scaffolding and covering it with decorative paper to add to the festive atmosphere when she heard a voice behind her.

"Hey MB," Josh said, as he approached the store.

"Hey back." She turned towards the voice and saw Josh approaching the shop empty-handed. She gave him a quizzical look.

"I made a small change in plans. I hope you don't mind."

"That depends on the change." Marybeth didn't like plans changing without warning.

"You have the final say," he said, picking up on her hesitation. "I haven't been staying at my mom's house this week. I wanted to be able to get some space and perspective on the whole task, and to be out of the way for the sale."

"Yeah?" Marybeth didn't like where this was going.

"I have a room at the bed and breakfast across the common."

"Yeah?"

Josh was starting to get nervous, sensing that his plan might not be going so well. "I was talking with the proprietor, Anna, today about our pumpkin carving evening and she invited us to carve over at the B&B. What do you think?"

She looked at him suspiciously but didn't say anything.

"It would be more comfortable than the back alley of the store. Anna said she'd set out some snacks and her signature Bailey's Cocoa Coffee to take the evening chill off. How can you turn that down?"

"Okay, but we're still not having sex at the end of the evening," she cautioned.

"Understood," he chuckled, "but once again I reserve the option to kiss you goodnight."

Marybeth resisted her immediate impulse to argue.

They locked up the shop and headed across the common. Josh took her hand as they walked. Marybeth immediately pulled it away.

"Sorry," he said apologetically. "Did I do something wrong?"

"No, it's not that. It's just a small town, people talk a lot. If someone sees us hand in hand headed to the B&B, the grapevine will be on fire by morning."

"And that would be terrible?" he asked sounding genuinely hurt.

"I don't know. I'm not ready to deal with that yet. My ex-husband already keeps the gossipers seriously

busy. It wouldn't take much to add me to the story lines.
So for now I would just like to lay low."

"Okay", Josh conceded. "But you'll have to tell me
more about it later."

"Only if I have to," Marybeth replied.

"You do."

They headed across the common to The Traveler's
Inn Bed and Breakfast. The Inn dated back to the
1800s, when it was a convenient stopover for travelers
on their way between Philadelphia and Harrisburg. It
served many different purposes over the years including
a boarding school for girls and a convalescent center for
WWII veterans. Its most recent incarnation was back to
its original use. The renovations were completed ten
years ago by a couple who retired from the corporate
world. The outside had a small front lawn and
landscaped back yard with a porch that wrapped around
the house on three sides. It was on this wrap-around
porch that Marybeth spotted the work area that had
been set up for the carving. Awaiting them was a
pumpkin of respectable size accompanied by various
sharp objects.

"Well, how'd I do?" Josh asked puffing his chest
up in mock pride.

"Impressive. You get an A. Do you have a backup
in case we screw it up?"

"We are not going to screw it up," Josh stated
confidently.

Marybeth spotted a small instruction book with
pattern suggestions. "Ah, I see you have done your best
to ensure that."

"Yes, indeed. I am not a risk taker. I believe in
having what I need for every task."

"And those?" Marybeth asked pointing to two

smaller pumpkins off to the side.

"I thought we might make smaller ones if we wanted to. You know, for the cause."

"For the cause," Marybeth smiled.

They spent the next hour and a half making design decisions and operating on their orange patients. The task flowed seamlessly, each anticipating the others next move. Her comfort around Josh sent off emotional alarms. She struggled to enjoy the moment and not allow her past pain to rule the day. Still, logic kept her skeptical about this man and his motivations. After all, he was leaving town next week probably for good, a fact that was never far from her awareness.

She was acutely aware of Josh's physical proximity. Their kiss had ignited a sexual energy in her that had been tucked neatly away along with painful emotions and other things-to-be-avoided. Marybeth could feel the electricity between them throughout her body. Again she felt that comfortable/uncomfortable dilemma. She had become a detached head walking around on a manikin. Their first kiss had reconnected the old circuitry with alarming force and was threatening to override all other systems. She assumed that Josh had also tuned into the energy by the way he lingered when he was closest to her. She wondered what was going through his mind.

Meanwhile Josh was trying to avoid his own demons. He was all too aware of his own awakening emotions that had long been tucked away out of sight. His heart had been left tired and ragged by his last relationship and he wasn't sure it was in any shape now to get back into the ring. He wasn't even interested in starting a relationship until he met Marybeth. Now, this physical energy between them was threatening to override the fortress protecting his heart. His mind wandered for a moment to the last conversation he had had with his mother before her fall. She said that he would meet a new love and suffer a loss. At the moment she was at least one for two.

It was near dark by the time they were done. Lighted candles were the final touch, testing the effect of their labor.

"See. Perfect." Josh made a grand presentation gesture.

"Lucky for you," Marybeth teased.

"No luck involved," he said, cleaning up the last of the pumpkin guts off the porch floor. "Are you ready for snacks and coffee?"

Marybeth's stomach growled. She put both hands on her belly, embarrassed by the noise.

"I guess I am."

"Let's go in and see what Anna set up. If it's not to your liking, we can order take-out or go somewhere for dinner." Josh blew out the candles as they headed inside.

Just beyond the entryway was a lovely sitting area decorated tastefully with simple furniture and a splash of Victorian lace here and there that gave it a sense of times past. On the side buffet table lay a delightful assortment of hors d'oeuvres and sweets. There were little quiches, brie and bread, and a crock pot with a little tent card that read Creamy Chicken Vegetable Soup. Just beyond the soup were bite-size cannolis and brownies. At the end of the line was a large urn with another tent card reading Decaf Bailey's Cocoa Coffee.

"Wow, this looks fabulous. Did she think she was feeding the masses?" Marybeth asked.

"I might have mentioned that it was a special

night," Josh replied coyly.

"Oh yeah?"

"Yeah. It's your second date in twenty-five years," Josh kidded.

"Fifteen", she corrected. "And is this really a date?"

"Absolutely. I picked you up. We went somewhere for an activity and dinner. And I will be kissing you good night."

"So you say," she countered. "Anyway, this looks great for me for dinner. What do you think?"

"It looks great to me too. Way more than I expected. "

They loaded up their plates and sat down at a small bistro table that looked out over the lighted back yard. By day, the back yard was a picture perfect garden with raised flowerbeds and stone paths. In the evening, it lit itself up with a fanciful display of lighted flowers, butterflies and fairies courtesy of little solar panels hidden in the plants. In addition to its regular decorative lighting, there were witches and trolls of various sizes and a large Jack-o-lantern in the fountain that had been shut off for the winter. It was a perfect setting for a quiet dinner for two.

"So, tell me what your ex-husband is up to that keeps the town gossips busy?" Josh inquired.

"Well, it seems he is reliving his youth or sewing his wild oats or something. The bottom line is that he has slept with half the single women in Pomroy and a few in Westfield since our divorce two years ago". She shook her head. "It was painful at first, I'm not going to lie. It felt like he was glad to be rid of me or that he was intentionally trying to hurt me, and maybe he was. Then I realized it was just his way to avoid being alone and I started to feel sorry for him. Different people would come up to me to let me know his newest interest. I had to ask people to stop telling me what he was doing."

"Sounds awkward," Josh sympathized.

"It is. It leaves me wondering what I ever saw in him. The whole marriage and divorce left me doubting myself in a lot of ways. For a long time, I struggled to make sense of it. Somewhere along the way I realized that it wasn't going to make sense, maybe ever, so I do my best to stay in the present moment, letting go of what he does or doesn't do."

"I understand what you mean about doubting yourself. I had a relationship that ended badly a few years ago. It completely blindsided me. One minute it was great. The next it was not. It went bad fast. It left me wondering what I missed."

"Oh, the quiet writer has a story of his own, does he?" Marybeth smiled quizzically. Their eyes met and lingered for a moment longer than necessary.

"We all have our stories, don't we," he replied.

"Yes, we do. And right now I want to hear some of yours."

"Yeah, well, fair's fair I guess," he hedged.

"Yes it is," she said, not letting him off the hook.

"A while back," he started.

"A while back, when?"

Josh realized he wasn't going to get away with too many generalities so he started again.

"Ten years ago if you go back to the beginning. I met a woman at a writing workshop. I had gotten tired of writing magazine articles and decided I wanted to try my hand at a novel, so I registered for a week-long workshop in Colorado to help get me started. I met her at the opening cocktail hour. She was a visual artist that was taking the course to learn how to illustrate books. We immediately connected and spent most of the week together, collaborating and spending spare time enjoying the area. She was originally from North Carolina but was living in Colorado at that time. We did the long distance thing for a few months but at the time neither one of us had the money to make that work for long."

"Long distance must be difficult...and pricey," she sympathized.

"It is. Then we decided to co-author a children's book, me writing the text and she doing the illustration. She would come stay with me in Connecticut while we completed the book and to see how things went between us. My understanding was that she was going to maintain her Colorado apartment, sublet maybe, until we had a chance to get to know each other better. A month later she showed up at my house with a pickup truck packed full with everything she owned."

"She did NOT!" Marybeth struggled to suppress a smile.

He looked up at Marybeth and smiled shaking his head. "I can laugh about it now, but at the time I was freaking out, thinking that somehow I had given her the wrong impression or that our wires had crossed somewhere. In hindsight, I realized that this was her standard MO. Anyway, I let her move in and things went well at first. The creative collaboration of our book was exciting and had a very intimate energy all its own. Our connection seemed to be almost telepathic about the book and life in general. We finished each other's sentences. We wanted the same thing for dinner."

Josh paused here, wandering off into his memories

for a moment.

"Leela's Lei," Marybeth inserted into his reflections.

He looked a little startled at first but then smiled. "I see you have been doing your research. What did you do, Google me?" he asked smiling.

"I might have," she replied joking back. "Technology is a great thing."

"Did you do a background check too?" he asked.

"No, but I did try to get your IRS records. Did you know that stuff is protected?" They both broke out laughing, lightening the moment.

"Good to know," he replied nodding his head. "I probably should have tried that with Jan."

Marybeth knew he was talking about Janet Morrison, the co-author of his book, but she didn't comment on it.

"Just so you know, I have not Googled you," Josh added.

"You won't find much. My life just isn't that exciting," she admitted.

"Oh, I don't know about that. Seems the last few weeks have been full of adventure," he said, reminding her of recent events.

"Yes, recently that would be true, but before that, pretty boring. So, what happened with Jan?"

Josh squirmed at being back in the spotlight. "A major publishing house picked up our book. We signed contracts and went into print. The publisher wanted us to do a lot of promotional events all over the East Coast, here one day, there the next. In hindsight, I think the stress was too much for Jan. It seemed that as long as her world was not very big or very complicated she was okay, but as soon as the stress level went up, she got really crazy. She would stay up all night worrying about things. She would imagine that I was trying to cheat her out of money or that I was having an affair. She was paranoid at times. There was no reasoning with her. I kept waiting for things to go back the way they were, for her to calm back down, but it never happened."

"I know that feeling."

"In the end, I probably stayed a little too long. When it finally blew up completely, there were police calls and restraining orders. Four and a half years from start to finish. It still confuses me when I think about it. And I try not to."

Marybeth could relate to the last comment. She worked hard not to think about things. It had served her well or so she thought, until that damn kiss.

They both knew that tomorrow would be a busy day. The evening would be the opening of the Jack-o-lantern festival and the following day would begin the two day estate sale. Marybeth took advantage of the excuse to end the evening early. It was about 9:00 when she made the first closing comments.

"Well, it's getting late for me. Why don't you bring the pumpkins by in the morning. I'll be there around 9:30 doing paperwork and working in the back."

"Yes, ma'am," he replied as he helped her into her jacket. He pulled her close and kissed her, then grabbed his own jacket. "I'll walk you to your car. That way I can kiss you again behind the store, well out of sight of the neighbors," he kidded.

"Maybe," she replied.

They walked back across the common, mostly in silence. Both reflecting on the evening's activities and conversation. As they headed around to the back of the building where Marybeth's car was parked, Josh took her hand. She didn't protest.

When they got to her car, Josh stepped quickly and obviously between Marybeth and the car, apparently afraid the window of opportunity might be small. They were both smiling at the maneuver.

"Worried?" Marybeth asked.

"No. Maybe a little," he laughed. Without saying another word, he reached up as he had done before and took her face gently in his hands. He slowly kissed her lips once, then again. The second one lasting longer than the first. When Marybeth didn't protest, Josh put his arms around her and gently pulled her body to his and pressed his lips just a little more firmly to hers. She gingerly put her arms around him, feeling a jolt of electricity throughout her body. It didn't last long. It didn't have to. They were both breathless as Josh stepped back to let her get into her car.

"Good night. See you tomorrow," he said.

"Good night" she replied as she slid into the driver's seat and closed the door. Josh backed slowly away from the car and watched her drive off before he headed back to the B&B.

Chapter 23

The next day Marybeth was busy getting ready for the festival. Her thoughts were distracted by the growing affection she was developing for Josh. He had come by first thing this morning to deliver the jack-o-lanterns with coffee and sweet rolls. After they shared coffee, he headed back to his mother's house to take care of some last minute things in preparation for the estate sale that would start tomorrow. Marybeth hadn't asked when he was leaving town. Asking would imply caring and she was doing her best not to. Josh hadn't brought it up either.

She spent the morning rearranging the storefront displays. The shop wouldn't be open tonight but she wanted to make the most of the crowds by presenting something interesting in the windows. She had just opened for the afternoon when the bell rang on the door to the shop and Eric walked in. He rarely came by and didn't make much of an attempt to contact her. She was fine with that. She didn't make the effort either. The divorce had been bitter and she had no desire to speak to him for any reason. But she knew him well enough to know that something was on his mind. Something big.

"Can I talk to you?" he asked.

"Sure. Go," she said with indifference.

"Not here, Marybeth. Can we go get a coffee at Jake's?"

Jake's was the local coffee shop and diner. She was reluctant to be seen in public with Eric lest anyone jump to any conclusions but she couldn't see a graceful way around it. It was after lunch and the diner wouldn't be very crowded. Whatever Eric had on his mind seemed important.

"Okay. Sure."

Marybeth had a sign on the door that read "Be back at" and it had a little clock you could adjust. She pointed the hands to read two o'clock and locked the door. They walked down to Jake's in silence. Neither one finding much to say to each other. What was there to say? He had cheated her out of the house and half of her retirement by manipulating his own bank accounts to reflect abject poverty, then requested spousal support. She could feel the fire rising within her as they approached Jake's.

They found a booth and ordered coffee. Marybeth was taking long deep breaths trying to keep her rage at bay.

"I have something to tell you." he started. "I'm sorry for the pain it will cause you." He watched her face closely for reactions. Marybeth held her breath. What could he possibly do to hurt her any more than he already had? She was completely unprepared for what came next.

"I'm having a baby with Joann Gleason." He stopped, waiting for a response.

Marybeth felt like she had been slapped in the face by God himself. How could this be happening? She and Eric had tried for years to have a baby without success. It was a constant sadness that hung over their marriage. A pain that few people understood. And here he was telling her that he was having a baby with the town tramp! She hated him more at this moment than she had ever hated anyone in her life. She hadn't noticed it but she was hyperventilating.

"I'm sorry. I'm sorry," he was saying as he reached out to touch her. She jerked her hands back as if he had the plague. Pain was taking over her entire being. She was completely speechless. She was sitting there with her mouth open, gasping for breath when the waitress brought over the coffee. She was a sweet young girl from the local high school. Marybeth knew her family casually. She tried to pull herself together enough to whisper out a thank you. Eric nodded to the girl as she walked away.

They sat in silence. Neither one knowing where to go next with this. Eric broke the impasse with, "I didn't know how else to tell you. I'm sorry. I knew it would be hard on you no matter what. We've been casually dating and . . . " Eric didn't get the last of the sentence out when Marybeth shot back.

"You mean casually *f-f-fucking*, don't you," she spat out with particular emphasis on the f. Eric winced. He had expected it. And maybe deserved it. He had tried to dress it up a little but truth is truth. His behavior of late was less than ideal. He watched as tears began to well up in her eyes.

Eric still loved her. He had been against the divorce from the beginning, wishing that they could work things out. He hadn't realized how bad his behavior had gotten till it was too late. Then he just got angry and wanted to hurt her in any way he could. He had made it hard on her. He knew that. But as much as he had wanted to get even back then, he never ever wanted to inflict this kind of pain on her.

"Get away from me," she said quietly, staring

down at her coffee.

Eric hesitated for a moment then started to protest.

"Get away from me," she repeated through clenched teeth.

Eric knew this was not the time to have any more conversation about it. He wanted to say more, to tell her how it had all gone down, to share his own panic at the situation, to be able to work through their old grief together. It still might happen, but not now. He left, paying for the coffee on the way out.

Marybeth sat in shock, overwhelmed with a twisting pain in her gut. She was literally frozen in place. If she could move, she knew it would take her out of this spiral of pain. Even a sip of coffee would pull her back into reality, but she was slipping too quickly into the abyss.

After some time, the young waitress came over and asked if she was okay. It shook Marybeth back into the present and she realized she was sobbing. She looked up at the waitress who was wide-eyed and about to panic. Marybeth took a deep breath and a long swig of coffee.

"I'm fine," she choked out.

"Can I get you anything?" the waitress asked timidly.

"No," she managed to whisper "Thank you." Marybeth gulped the rest of the coffee and left the café.

On autopilot, she headed back to the shop. As she walked, rage started to replace pain. It started deep in her gut and rose through her body like a slow wave of fire that she was not sure she could contain. When she got back to the shop, she went around back to her car and drove herself home. Next thing she knew, she was unlocking her back door. She didn't actually remember much after leaving the café.

She gasped out a breath as she entered her house. Had she held her breath all the way home? Maybe. She stumbled in and headed for the sink thinking she was going to vomit, but the wave was not one of nausea. It was rage and pain. The rage that had been staved off at the café came on in full force and what spewed from her mouth was a blood curdling, earth shattering scream that came from the core of her being.

"NNNNNNNNOOOOOOOOOOOOOOOOOOOO!! !!!!!!!!!!"

Sobbing uncontrollably, she made her way to the couch. The pain was blinding. Every muscle in her body was cringing, contorting her into an almost fetal position. As she brought her head up to let loose another bellow, she spotted the music box still sitting on the coffee table. She picked up the happy couple with all her might she hurled it at the stone fireplace. She fell to her knees just as the object hit the stone. Damn that thing for making her feel sorry of Eric, that bastard! She threw Josh in there too – the out-of-town interloper trying to break down her defenses! Fuck them all!

She watched as the porcelain shattered into a hundred pieces. It made no sound and appeared to be happening in slow motion, like she was out of sync with time. It gave off a shimmering glow that she instantly recognized as one of those strange visions. Dear God, she thought, not now, but before the thought was even complete, a warm white glow settled over the living room and a sense of peace filled her so completely she wondered if she was dead. As she watched, the light began to focus in front of the fireplace. In the center appeared the woman from her previous vision of the church. The woman spoke with great compassion, her arms extended with palms up in the pose of saints.

"Dear beautiful Marybeth, you are a great manifestation of God, perfect in every way. You chose to come into this lifetime to minister to parents and children. You knew you would not bear your own. You chose this so you could be more helpful to others. As hard as it is to believe right now, you will help Eric as well, to love and care for this new life he is now responsible for. He will need you. This baby will need you. Do not despair. Your life is perfect, your service to humanity is great. With each small act of kindness, you move people to experience the joy of life. With every laugh, you lift up a soul who has fallen. This is your purpose and you are fulfilling it perfectly."

Before Marybeth could argue, the vision faded off and she was alone in her living room. The remains of the music box gave off one final note as it lay on the stone hearth.

She sat there stunned. Numb. Confused. Surely the woman in the vision couldn't be right. That would just be too cruel. What now? What should she do? She looked around internally for her rageful, self-righteousness but couldn't find it. Taking its place was deep profound sorrow.

She needed coffee. She went into the kitchen and made a fresh pot. As she wandered around the kitchen, she spotted the tarot cards sitting on the kitchen table. She poured her coffee without waiting for the pot to finish and sat down. Staring at the deck, she began an internal dialog with herself about the irrationality of tarot cards. It was all just random, right? The card the other day, the two of cups, just random. And what if she pulled one now? It wouldn't mean anything, right? Just random. Before she knew it, she was gently unwrapping the scarf to expose the deck of cards. She spread them out, face down, in an arc across the kitchen table and stared at them. Oh, what the heck. She selected a card and turned it over. King of Swords. She studied the card for a moment and then reached for the book.

King of Swords indicates a man who is intelligent, subtle and clever. He is also highly intuitive and perceptive. His nature will be elusive and ethereal, yet he has a strength and fascination that is hard to deny. Because of the inquiring and analytic nature of his mind, you will often find him involved in mystical study, and following spiritual pursuits. He cuts through the confusion and provides clarity. He is honorable, truthful and reliable. He is impartial and just. He lives by the highest ethical standards.

Could this be Josh? What if it was? Just then the phone rang.

"Hello," Marybeth stammered into the phone.

"MB. Are you all right?" Josh was almost shouting with concern.

"Yes, I'm okay, I guess," she replied.

"Where are you? I'm at the shop and the sign says you'll be back two hours ago?"

"I'm home," was all she could muster.

He sensed something was definitely wrong. "I'll be right there."

Marybeth didn't argue.

When Josh arrived, she was sitting on the couch in the living room with a cup of coffee and a shattered mess on the floor by the fireplace. She looked stunned. He sat down beside her, took her hand and gently but directly asked, "What happened?"

Marybeth, slowly putting her thoughts together, told him everything, starting from Eric's visit and ending with the vision of the woman in the green veil. Most of the time she was staring off, as if she were reading the information from some screen inside her head. "Now I'm sure I'm going crazy," she said flatly.

He reached out and put his arms around her. "You are a brilliant beautiful woman and you are not going crazy," he said as he pulled her close to him. "You are simply waking up." She willingly turned to him and accepted the comfort of his arms, resting her head on his shoulder, wondering how much more she could take.

Chapter 24

They sat that way for a long time in silence. Finally, without a word, Josh gently rose from the couch, picked up Marybeth's coffee cup and headed to the kitchen. He came back out in a moment with two cups of coffee and some cookies he found on the counter. Still shocked by the afternoon's events, Marybeth gratefully accepted the coffee and cookies, surprised at how well Josh knew her already. With a flash of anger at herself, she realized how vulnerable she'd become. But she no longer had the energy or inclination to push people away.

Finally Josh broke the silence. "Will people be expecting to see you tonight?"

"Well, let's just say my absence would be noticed," she replied staring at her coffee. "Especially since half the town knows about this pregnancy already and the other half will know by the end of the night."

"Seriously?" Josh asked.

"Yeah, seriously," she answered.

"Okay then, let's dress up and show up," Josh said trying to lighten the mood.

"Yes, I suppose so." She was starting to move out of numbness and into reality.

"Sure. Go put on something that looks hot and let's give 'em something to talk about."

"I don't own anything that looks hot," she lamented.

"Sure you do," he said smiling. "You were wearing it the other night."

"Really? I think that's a stretch but I'll go put it on. You're right, I suppose. I'll have to face people sooner or later. Might as well get it over with."

She disappeared into the back and returned in the same form-fitting knit top and scarf, trading in the black chinos and pumps for blue jeans tucked into knee high leather boots. She grabbed a short leather jacket as they headed for the door. She noticed Josh looking her up and down.

"Yeah, that's the look," he said, smiling as they headed out the door.

Josh drove them back to the B&B where he changed into his own look for the night. Marybeth waited in the sitting room where they had eaten dinner the night before. It seemed like a long time ago now. Josh reappeared with a hot look all his own, in a button-down forest green denim shirt with a few buttons opened at the chest, khakis and a soft leather blazer. They looked each other up and down and started laughing. It felt good to laugh and Marybeth was extremely grateful at this moment for Josh's upbeat attitude. They grabbed some of the house specialty Bailey's Cocoa Coffee and headed out the door.

They paused on the porch to survey the landscape. The entire common was aglow with shelf after shelf, row after row of Jack-o-lanterns. If there was a flat surface, there was a pumpkin on it. Big and small, scary and funny. This year some creative minds had carved their names into them or other short messages. It was truly an amazing sight and Josh was significantly impressed by the effect.

As they walked into the night, Marybeth took a deep breath and braced herself for the comments, questions and sympathetic looks from friends and acquaintances. She accepted the arm offered by Josh and walked tall out into the crowds. It was only a matter of seconds when the owner of the shop next to her came running up to them. "Wow, Marybeth. Sorry to hear about Eric, honey. How are you doing?" She gave Marybeth a hug.

"Thanks Diane. I'm fine," Marybeth replied.

"And who is your date?" Diane countered, changing the topic and cocking her head towards Josh.

"This is Josh. He's a friend from out of town. Josh, this is Diane. She owns the store next to mine."

"Nice to meet you, Diane," Josh smiled.

Diane smiled big and looked him up and down. "You gonna be in town long, Josh?"

There it was, the question they were both avoiding. Josh stammered a moment. "Just a few more days," he said, feeling as if the air had been sucked out of his lungs.

"Too bad. Well, have fun tonight," she said as she headed on towards the end of the common where the opening ceremonies would be held.

They looked at each other for a long moment.

"I guess we have to talk about that sooner or later," Josh offered. Then he reached out and pulled Marybeth into a huge bear hug. Marybeth went agreeably into his arms. To hell with the townspeople.

"I vote for later," she said. She just wanted to get through the evening and take advantage of Josh's company and support.

"Understood," Josh replied.

They headed back out into the crowd.

Just as Marybeth had predicted, many people commented on the latest news story in town. Others shared sympathetic looks from across the crowd. Eric and Joann were there of course. The whole town was. They managed to keep their distance although Eric seemed particularly interested in who Marybeth was with.

"Hey, MB!" Angie called out as she approached them. "Good to see you out tonight, especially considering the news. And lookin' so hot, too. You go girl," she said as she looked them both up and down, smiling. Just then two monsters and a fairy princess came running out of the crowd and grabbed hold of Angie's legs and hands.

"Mom, where did you go?!" one demanded.

"I'm right here fairy princess," she replied. Then, to Marybeth and Josh, she joked, "I've been trying to lose them all night".

"How hard can it be?" Marybeth joked back.

"Are you kidding? They're like little homing pigeons!" They all laughed and once again Marybeth felt a lightness returning to her heart.

"We're headed down to the front to watch them light the big guy. We saw them hoist it up this afternoon. Wanna come with?" Angie invited.

"No thanks. We'll watch from here," Marybeth assured her.

"Suit yourself," she replied and off she went like the Pied Piper. As she walked away, Marybeth couldn't help but notice the spring in her step that hadn't been there before. She knew the message from Jackie had changed things for the better and she was grateful she could be part of it.

They walked around enjoying all the costumes and food. They listened and cheered as the Master Jack-o-lantern was ceremonially lit. Then, when Marybeth had had enough for one night, they headed back to the B&B looking for more specialty coffee and some heat. The night had turned cold and she was remembering that looking hot seldom equated with being warm.

They sat quietly on the couch, neither one wanting to bring up the topic of Josh's departure. It was Josh who started.

"I've been in touch with my brother and my cat sitter. My brother needs me to finish signing off on some paperwork. My cat has apparently disowned me and put an ad on Craig's List for a new person," he smiled, trying to lighten the conversation. It didn't work.

"Look, I've known you were just passing through all along. So, no big deal. When are you heading out?" Marybeth replied sounding a little more snippy than she wanted to. She was angry at herself for caring.

"No. You look, MB. I'm not the 'just passing through' kinda guy," he replied looking straight into her eyes. She looked away. He gently turned her face back towards his. "I don't know what's happening between us, MB, but I'm not willing to blow it off as some time filler while I'm here on other business."

"Well, how do you know it's not? Maybe I'm just a distraction from your grief over your mother's death," Marybeth blurted out thoughtlessly.

Josh took a long slow breath. "Really? Is that what you think this is?"

It was Marybeth's turn to pause. "I don't know. At this moment, I don't see how it can be much of anything. You live in Connecticut! And you are leaving in four days to go home!"

"And I am sorry that that's true. But I'm interested in seeing what this can be, and not in writing it off as some casual something. Because it's not casual for me. You are the first woman in years who has sparked any feelings at all and I'm not sure I want to let a few miles decide how it goes."

"Isn't this feeling a little like déjà vu for you? You know, meet someone while away from home, carry on long distance, till...." she let it trail off regretting it as soon as it was out of her mouth.

"Don't you think I am aware of that? I've been chewing on that since the day I met you, wondering if this is just the same..." It was his turn to leave the thought unfinished. "But I don't think it is."

"What makes this different?" she challenged.

"Because I'm different."

"I don't know," Marybeth insisted. "I just don't know. I don't know. I don't know!"

Josh took her hand. "I don't know either. Don't you want to find out?"

"I don't know," she replied quietly, looking away from him.

"I know you're scared," he started, but Marybeth cut him off.

"The hell I am," she shot back.

"Really?" he asked with that 'who are you trying to convince' look on his face.

She took a deep breath. "I guess I'm angry that my heart keeps overriding my brain." She could feel her emotions forcing their way to the surface. "Up until four weeks ago, my life was pretty predictable. Then I meet this crazy old woman at a freakish yard sale and my life is upside down. Then you wander into my

forever-altered reality! I'm still think I might be crazy."
She pulled her hand away from his. She got up abruptly
and headed over to the coffee. Her mind was racing
with thoughts of all the shit she put up with from Eric,
all the promises, all the lies. Then she added the crazy
visions, the information from her parents and Grams, all
of it. It was just too much at this moment.

Josh got up and followed her to the coffee. He
walked up behind her, put his arms around her and held
their bodies together. Marybeth gave in and allowed
him to cradle her for a moment.

"I'm sorry," she said quietly. "I guess all this stuff
with Eric has brought up huge piles of garbage for me."
She turned to face him and before she could say another
word, Josh was kissing her and her heart took over
completely.

They kissed for a long time, both surrendering to
the moment, saving caution and logic for another day.
When they finally released each other, Josh was the
first to break the mood. "You've had one hell of a day
and we have an estate sale tomorrow. As much as I hate
to say this, let me take you home."

Chapter 25

The estate sale was busy from the get-go. Marybeth had hired a few people to help out with the cash register and monitoring the house. It wasn't long before things were headed out the front door. She noticed a pained look cross Josh's face.

"Are you okay?"

"Yeah. It's just very weird seeing my mother's things sold off to strangers."

"I can't imagine it." She slipped one arm around his back and snuggled in beside him. He responded with an arm over her shoulder, pulling her close to him.

"How am I going to do this, MB?" he said, looking off into the distance.

"I imagine it will get easier as the day goes on."

'No. Not this." He waved his arm to include the house. "This." He pulled her in closer, putting both arms around her. "Leaving."

She took a deep breath. "Well, I take comfort in knowing that it's not easy for you." She smiled up at him. He kissed her.

"I'm glad it makes you feel better."

"Hey, MB, Josh. Sorry to interrupt." It was Angie calling from across the room. "There's someone asking about the

Mustang." She was waving at them and pointing with her head at the woman standing beside her.

"And here we go." Josh took a deep breath and headed across the room.

At the end of the two days, most of the big items had sold. The electronics went fast, mostly due to certificates Josh had gotten from a local computer shop. A book dealer had taken all the books. An art auction house had purchased three quarters of the artwork. The Mustang was purchased as a college graduation present for the woman's son.

"So what now?" Marybeth and Josh were sitting on the front steps catching their breath at the end of the day. Marybeth was waiting for an answer.

"I'm not sure why you think I have any answers here."

"One of us should know what we're doing."

"Okay. I suggest it's you."

"Oh, no. I had to take charge in my marriage. I'm not doing it now." Marybeth was shaking her head for emphasis.

"I'm not suggesting that you take charge. I'm just saying I don't know."

"Somebody has to know."

"Why?"

She hesitated. "Because it feels too scary to not know."

He slid closer to her. "We'll just have to make it up as we go."

"Easy for you to say."

"Not really, no. But I don't have an alternative. And I think we're both too tired to have this conversation right now."

"I'm sure you're right. I know I'm exhausted."

"We still have a couple of days. Let's do this in the morning."

"Agreed."

They walked to her car, arm in arm and lingered over one last kiss before Marybeth headed home.

Flopping on the couch as soon as she walked in the door, she kicked off her shoes and closed her eyes. But something was nagging at her. She sat up and looked around. The Box caught her eye, still tucked in the corner of the room. It seemed like a lifetime ago that she first acquired it and in some ways it was. Her entire life had been rewritten since her first encounter with the old woman. Things had gotten so busy between the estate sale and the Jack-o-lantern Festival that she had almost forgotten about it. Now, even through her exhaustion, her curiosity got the best of her and she pulled it out of the corner.

Sitting on top was the old family photo. She picked it up. Nothing happened, for which she was grateful. She knew she was done with it. She smiled as she remembered the words of the old woman when Marybeth had asked for the items. "I'm done with them," she had said. Marybeth had thought it an odd statement at the time. Now she understood. But it left her wondering what to do next.

She considered putting it on her mantle or sticking it in a drawer somewhere but it felt weird having someone else's family portrait in the house. She wasn't feeling any sentimental attachment to it despite its impact on her life but throwing it away didn't seem right either. It had a lovely old-fashioned frame so she decided to put it in the shop.

She noticed the last item in The Box. It was the prayer book. She considered picking it up but knew she was too tired to risk any strangeness tonight. She resolved to deal with it after Josh had left town. She just didn't have the energy for any more funny business.

Chapter 26

The next morning, Marybeth headed off to the shop as usual. And as usual, Angie was already there. Even though she had not gone yard saleing that weekend, she had picked up a few items left over from Josh's sale thinking they might sell in the shop over the next couple of weeks. On top of a pile of knickknacks was the framed family from The Box.

"What's with this?" Angie asked.

"I thought the frame might sell. It's old and a little unusual" Marybeth replied.

"Okay, I'll put it out, photo and all. It will sell better with something in it," she said as she picked it up. Marybeth froze for a moment wondering what mojo the thing still had. Apparently, none at the moment and Angie headed to the front of the shop. She found a blank tag under the register and wrote "Instant Ancestors $10". She attached the label to the photo and placed it on the shelf behind the register, then returned to the back to sort through the rest of the items.

Marybeth was out at the register when Josh showed up bearing coffee and sweet rolls. He came in with a smile and a big "Good Morning." As he approached the register, his expression changed and his pace slowed. His eyes went back and forth from the picture on the shelf to Marybeth.

"Where did you get that?" he asked slowly.

She turned to see what he was looking at.

"Why?" She wasn't sure she liked his tone.

Josh paused for a moment trying to reorganize something in his head.

"That's my mother's family portrait," he said softly with a look of curiosity and confusion.

"What?" Now, it was her turn to pause for mental reorganizing. "That's the picture I got from the old woman at the yard sale. She said she was the middle child." She shook her head quickly a few times as if the movement would somehow assist in fitting this information in somewhere.

"That's my mother's family," Josh repeated.

"It's not possible," was all she could come up with in reply.

They looked at each other is silence for what seemed like a long time. Had Josh's mother been the woman at the yard sale who left these items for Marybeth?

"Exactly when did this yard sale happen?"

"September thirteenth. I clearly remember the date," she said.

"My mother died on September eleven," he said flatly.

"It can't be," Marybeth whispered.

"Apparently it can." Josh raised his eyebrows. "I always knew my mother was an extraordinary woman, although I'm the first to admit this is a bit over the top."

"Hey MB? What do you want to do with. . ." Angie came bombing around the corner from the back room. As soon as she saw the looks on their faces, she stopped in her tracks. Clearly she was interrupting something big.

"Wow. Okay. I'm backing up now." She held her

hands in the air as if someone was holding a gun on her as she retreated backwards from whence she came. As she rounded the corner and out of site, she called out "I have to run an errand. I'll be back later," and headed out the back door.

They looked at each other and both burst out laughing. Simultaneously, they each reached for their coffee as if a little caffeine could help explain the present moment. They drank in silence, looking at each other, then at the photo, then back at each other, allowing their brains to make sense of the new information.

"Tell me about the yard sale."

Marybeth picked up the photo and headed to the sofa. "Let's sit down."

Josh grabbed the sweet rolls and sat down beside her. Marybeth proceeded to tell Josh the entire story of the yard sale in great detail. When she was done, Josh stared at the family photograph he now held in his hand. "So that must be the story of my mother's little sister. No one ever talked about it," Josh mused. "What happened to the prayer book?"

"It's still in The Box at my house."

"Can we go see it?"

Marybeth was reading his mind. "I'll lock up."

They drove in silence, both caught up in their own thoughts. As they pulled up in the driveway, they looked at each other, took a deep breath and got out of the car.

Josh sat on the couch as Marybeth retrieved The Box from the corner. She lifted the book out and set it on the coffee table. It was wrapped up in the cloth it had been resting on at the yard sale. They looked at each other then at the book.

    Josh slowly reached out for the book. As soon as he
had it firmly in his hands, he froze. She knew the look.
Josh was having a vision.

                          * * *

    Suddenly Josh felt himself pulled into another
place. He saw his mother in the kitchen getting a
snack together for him. He saw himself come in
from school angry and tearful. It was the day the
girl had collapsed.

    "Oh my, what's wrong?" she had asked
instantly.

    "I'm just the biggest freak this town has ever
seen, that's all."

    "What happened?"

    "It's these stupid colors I see!"

    Mom put a hand on his shoulder. "Sit down
and tell me what happened."

    Josh watched his mother nodding
encouragement as he related the story.

    "None of the girls will come near me and half
of the boys won't either. I'll never have a girlfriend
now. I'll have the life of a freak!" he screamed
through tears.

    She put her arms around him and held him
close. "I know it doesn't feel good right now, but
this will pass and you will have a wonderful
girlfriend soon."

    "No, I won't," he insisted.

    "I know you will. Let's see." And she reached
over for her deck of cards. She pulled three.

    "One for past, one for present, one for future."

    Josh knew how his mother used the cards
and he knew that she was right a lot of the time.

    "See here, the past says that your true friends
will stand by you and false friends will be left
behind. The present says there will be a lot of

emotional upheaval. The future, look the Two of Cups, says that there will be a perfect match for you who will accept you completely just as you are." His mother looked up from the cards and into his eyes. "Don't worry. It will happen," she assured him.

* * *

He shook his head gently, momentarily disoriented. When he looked up at Marybeth, his face was wet with tears. "Sorry," he said, wiping his face.

"Don't be ridiculous. You have nothing to apologize for."

"Now I know what you mean, wondering if you're crazy. That was a little disturbing."

"You can talk about it if you like."

"It was a vision of my mom, when I was a kid, after the incident at school I told you about. I had forgotten that she pulled cards that day for me. One of them was the Two of Cups." He paused. She immediately made the connection to the card she pulled at the house that first day.

"Wow, imagine that." She looked into his eyes, smiling gently. They both chuckled.

Josh looked down at the book then opened the cover. The inside title page read *The Divine Feminine.* There was a hand-written inscription on the inside cover.

"Seek love, celebrate love, embrace love. Love is all there is – Mom," he read aloud.

"Is that your mother's handwriting?" Marybeth asked with a nervous jitter in her voice.

Josh nodded silently and turned the page again. Marybeth gasped. On the second page was the image of a beautiful dark woman wearing a green veil with gold trim. Under the image it read *Virgin de Guadalupe.*

"What is it?" Josh asked.

"It's the woman from my visions," Marybeth replied.

The full title of the book read "Worship of the Divine Feminine." It was a compilation of songs, prayers and stories since the beginning of time devoted to divine female energy from all religions and disciplines. Josh sat quietly, tears in his eyes, finally allowing the grief he had been keeping at bay to flow freely. Marybeth sat quietly beside him.

Epilogue

MARYBETH

It took Marybeth the better part of a year to integrate in all the new information and experiences of that Fall. It was amazing to her now how narrow her mind had been. She had a new respect for the people in her life, even Eric, who was proving to be the most neurotic father she had ever seen. She was beginning to understand the divine wisdom of the universe and no longer considered the events of her life to be tragic or unfair. Once she let go of all that, she was able to find joy in most things or, if not joy, at least a good laugh.

She and Josh traveled back and forth as often as they could. In between visits, they would have video chats or phone calls daily. Occasionally he came down for a week at a time and would work from her house.

She decided not to return to teaching, opting to maintain the store for the present. She enjoyed the low stress and freedom it allowed her. She continued to enjoy the creative process of repairing and re-purposing things. She felt like there was something more she had to do, in that cosmic kind of way, but she wasn't sure what it was and she was content to wait for clarity.

JOSH

Josh stayed those last few days at Marybeth's house.

They didn't leave each others side. Two days later, Josh reluctantly went back to Connecticut but not before making plans for Marybeth to visit his place in Connecticut in two weeks (minus the U-Haul). They realized it wasn't that far after all. Josh found a great place at the beach in New Jersey, which was a great half way point. They grew closer with each meeting, slowly, cautiously falling in love.

Finally able to move on from the past, he committed to a new relationship with Marybeth. He went on to write his next book, a novel for adolescents about growing up different.

ANGIE

The Board of Directors for the Franklin County Women's shelter invited Marybeth to take the seat vacated by Josh's mom. She declined, preferring to continue her support as she had been doing. She suggested Angie might be a good fit.

Happily accepting the position, she quickly became a force to be reckoned with. Through Angie's persistence, the mayors of the local towns got together to establish another shelter called Jackie's House. She was also a powerful advocate with the local police departments, offering monthly updates directly to the officers about shelter services and available space. She requested that she be notified of all domestic violence calls and began generating statistics used both locally and by national organizations. She also initiated training for officers on how to best support victims of abuse, how to identify hidden abuse and how to intervene effectively and legally. She spoke with the local judges and helped to institute mandated counseling for abusers and free counseling for victims.

An endowment from Josh's mother established a small memorial for anyone who died as a result of domestic abuse. The memorial sits on the courthouse property with Jacqueline Ann Delgato as the first name listed. A fund was set up to pay for the additions and maintain the memorial over time.

Angie placed an ad in the local papers requesting names and stories of loved ones lost to domestic violence. It was picked up by a Philadelphia paper and the response was overwhelming. With assistance from Josh, Angie put together a book to honor their stories.

REGINA

Regina couldn't get the words of the vision out of her mind. *"Your sister needs you now to show her how to be happy and have fun again. This is your job in this life, little one, to help your sister and others to laugh."* She developed a stand-up routine about divorced family dynamics of all things, and tried it out at a couple of the local bars. It met with such success that she started to play a few of the comedy clubs in Philly. Although her family was a little hesitant at first, they soon learned to laugh along with her at their antics over the years.

She married Tony and eventually worked out a routine on cohabiting vs. marriage that was equally successful. Tony was a good sport about being part of the joke, becoming a mini-celeb in his own right.

MOM

As a result of Marybeth's questions and conversations, Mom began to look at her own life with a different perspective. She had long conversations with Grams about how reckless a child she had been and regretted being so hard on Grams and Gramps. She gained a new respect for them and apologized for her harsh judgments. Mom and Grams made a plan to get together for brunch once a month to make the most of the time they had left together.

DAD

Dad started to experience some distress after talking about his time in the Army and his return home. He knew it was just old stuff that needed clearing up. He didn't waste any time. He started therapy again and was happy to find that treatment for PTSD had come a long way over the years. He began to feel better quickly. While at the VA, he bumped into one of his old military buddies. They reconnected with a few others and started meeting up regularly for golf or poker night. They didn't talk about the old days. They didn't have to. It was an unspoken bond they all understood.

Over the next year no one talked much about the events of that Autumn. There was simply an understanding between them all about the strange things that had occurred which changed their lives forever. Until one day Marybeth spotted a peculiar sign for a yard sale late in the day. . .

Afterthoughts

This story came about as the result of a lighthearted conversation with the minister of Unity Church on the west side of Albuquerque, New Mexico. Thanks Deb. This book is completely fictitious. Sort of. The stories and characters touch us all because the human experience is a common one. Here's some of the truth.

There is a Jack-o-lantern festival that happens every fall in New Hampshire. Previously held in Keene, it moved to Laconia in 2015. The event has broken several Guinness world records. It is a delightfully fun event in a lovely New England town. Go see it if you can. https://www.nhpumpkinfestival.com

----

The statistics around domestic violence are staggering. One out of every four women who are the victims of domestic violence attempt suicide. **On average, more than three women and one man are murdered by their intimate partners in this country every day.** Women account for 85% of the victims of intimate partner violence, men for approximately 15%. Women of all races are equally vulnerable to violence by an intimate partner. Intimate partner violence affects people regardless of income. **Nearly three out of four (74%) Americans personally know someone**

who is or has been a victim of domestic violence. In a national survey of American families, 50% of the men who frequently assaulted their wives also frequently abused their children. Why isn't there more of an outcry? If you would like to share a story of a loved one effected by domestic abuse, please go to our Facebook page

The Last Yard Sale

https://www.facebook.com/The.Last.Yard.Sale/

We like to think that we learned a lot from Vietnam about how to care for our returning soldiers. Sadly, that is often not the case and mental health issues go unreported and untreated. If you want to share stories of World War II, Vietnam or other combat trauma, either as a Vet or as a family member, please go to our Facebook page at

The Last Yard Sale

https://www.facebook.com/The.Last.Yard.Sale/

Fertility treatment can be a grueling ordeal. In many ways it takes the magic out of the moment. Adoption can be equally heartbreaking. If you would like to share words of encouragement or stories about infertility, please go to our Facebook page at

The Last Yard Sale

https://www.facebook.com/The.Last.Yard.Sale/

We often overlook how events from our childhood effected us then and now. Divorce is certainly one of those things. How much do we really understand at five or eight or ten years old? Life simply moves forward. If you'd like you can share your stories of a divorce as you saw it as a child at

The Last Yard Sale
https://www.facebook.com/The.Last.Yard.Sale/

Author's Note

This story isn't only about Marybeth and Josh. It's about an old woman who needs to let go of the last of her attachments to this life so she can move on to the next. The Last Yard Sale grew out of a short story I wrote as a spiritual exercise in letting go of that which no longer serves us. I hope it encourages you to let go of your own things - sooner than later.

About the Author

Marie LeClaire has spent the past thirty years as a mental health counselor encouraging others to look beyond our sometimes limited perspective and see a bigger picture of what influences our lives and guides our behavior. She has been writing novels and short stories for the past five years. She still does a little counseling part time but her love now is purely fiction - sort of. After all, art imitates life, doesn't it? Wandering around much of her adult life, she currently calls Virginia Beach, VA, home.

The Next

Last Yard Sale

It was a beautiful Saturday afternoon in October and MB was on her way home from a full day of yard saleing as usual. Her shop, One Woman's Junque: An Antique Boutique featured recreated and re-purposed items that other people didn't want. She had gained a bit of local fame and her shop appeared on the blogs of a few travelers who stumbled into the small town of Pomroy, an hour and a half outside of Philadelphia. They were mostly folks who wanted to escape the city and spend a few days in quieter surroundings. She knew her store offered a nice alternative to the local antique market and people seemed to appreciate her creative use of cast off items. Generally, she used the drive home to begin the creative process of transforming trash to treasure. Today however, she was a little preoccupied.

Josh was arriving in town on Tuesday. She hated to admit how much she looked forward to his visits. She wondered if she was just setting herself up for ultimate disappointment. How long had they been doing the long distance romance now? It had been almost a year! Where did the time go? Events of the past twelve months began flooding into her mind as if they had been perched on the edge of her awareness waiting for a chance to charge in.

It didn't surprise her. She worked hard to push them

aside, not sure how much to believe of her own memories. It all began with a strange yard sale and four peculiar items. There was the doll that had helped to rekindle her relationship with Regina. And the wedding couple music box that had played the song from her wedding and prompted her to get honest about her marriage and divorce. The family photograph that took her down the road of her own family history. And lastly, the book with it's message for Josh on the inside cover. And that wasn't even the bizarre part.

It was the old woman and the crazy visions that went along with the stories that she mostly tried not to think about. It all seemed hazy to her, even now. Thankfully, whatever had happened last fall had stopped as mysteriously as it had started and things had returned to normal in the blink of an eye. Sort of.

Giving in to the mental intrusion, she attended to the memories that were demanding to be heard. Trying to put them in order, she realized that the whole series of events had begun right around this time last year. Yes, it was a beautiful Fall day just like today. She had been on her way home from yard saleing when she had spotted one more yard sale sign and she just couldn't pass it up. In fact, it might have been this exact weekend. She thought it was unusual that she would be remembering things on just this day. Had her memories somehow conspired to remind her of the date?

The strange events of a year ago were kicked off by the ghost of Josh's mother and a yard sale from beyond the grave. She physically shuttered at the thought of it. Time gave her the luxury of rationalizing it away as a vivid dream or an overactive imagination. But her relationship with Josh had come out of that moment and there certainly was no dismissing that as imagination.

Was there? For a brief moment reality became confusing just as it had a year ago.

MB shook her head trying to shake away the memories.

"Focus on your driving before you kill yourself or someone else," she admonished herself out loud, shifting her attention to the drive home. "Right now I need to figure out how to get home."

She began to mentally plot her drive back to the house from her current location.

"Let's see, I think this road will take me back to Bramble Road then to Rt. 10, then to Main Street." She was pretty sure of it. Then she saw it, on an empty stretch of road. She knew it in her gut long before she got close enough to read it. It was a Yard Sale sign. Not any yard sale sign. *The* Yard Sale sign. The same sign she had spotted a year ago under just these circumstances. She felt a knot in her stomach begin to tighten up.

She instantly decided to pass it by. After all, she didn't have to stop at every sign she saw. Especially this one. Life had settled down nicely and she wasn't going to go looking for trouble. She drove past the sign.

"See," she said to the air, "I don't have to stop and I'm not going to."

Just as she was feeling empowered, she saw the same sign at the next side street.

"I will not turn. I will not turn," she told herself, fighting off the urge to do just that. "Let someone else stop."

She drove past the sign. As she rounded the next twist in the road, there it was again, at the end of a rural country lane.

"Damn!" she shouted as she banged on the steering

wheel. She pulled over and stopped on the shoulder. She stared at the sign, getting angry.

"Why me!?" she demanded.

"I won't!" she yelled at the sign. It seemed to stare back at her mockingly.

She thought about the old woman. Then about Josh. Truth was, her life had gotten significantly better since that yard sale a year ago and so had the lives of others. But things had just finally calmed down and she was looking forward to a normal life again.

"Damn," she said again with resignation as she slowly made the turn down the small road. She followed it around a few curves, past a couple of houses set back from the road. She was thinking that she might just be off the hook when a small house appeared at the end of the road with a table on the lawn. Pulling up in front of the house, she got out and looked around for the old woman. She didn't see anyone. She was about to make a quick get-away when a young man came out of the house. He stood on the stoop looking at her, hands in his pockets. He was wearing a green army tee shirt. His dog tags hung low around his neck. His green army pants were tucked into black boots. It was plain army green, not like the ones today that looked like desert camouflage. He looked to be about 20 and had a slightly timid demeanor.

"Afternoon, Ma'am," he greeted her.

"Good Afternoon," MB replied. "I was expecting an old woman."

"Yes, Ma'am. She told me you'd come by."

"Oh, she did, did she?" Irritation was creeping into her voice.

"Yes, Ma-am.".

"Oh, great." Her hackles were up now. "What do I

have, some kind of reputation in the afterlife now?"

"I can't say, Ma-am. She just said that you might be able to help."

MB let out a huff. "Very well then," she resigned herself to the situation and her attitude turned a bit kinder. "What do you think I can do for you?"

"Well, Ma-am, I have a couple of things that I need to get rid of." He nodded his head toward the table. MB turned to look. On the table sat two items, an army helmet and a stack of papers tied together with string. They were sitting close to each other as if they belonged together.

"Are you a soldier?" she asked, turning back to the young man.

"Yes, ma-am. At least I was. I don't recall much except that I have these things that I don't need anymore." Again he indicated the table with the nod of his head.

MB walked slowly over the the table while her insides argued about whether to run away or stay the course. When she got to the table, she looked up at the man who had asked for her assistance. She noticed again his almost childlike appearance, barely a man, really. Too young, she thought, to be dead.

"Is it okay if I pick them up?" She knew it would be the point of no return.

"Yes, ma-am."

She reached down to pick up the helmet and braced herself for what she suspected was coming. And she was right.

***

Suddenly, reality got all fuzzy and she found herself in what appeared to be an army compound. A transport truck carrying twenty or so soldiers was headed out of the yard. The young man from the porch was holding on to the side of the truck and reaching out the back, accepting a helmet from a soldier on the ground just out of sight.

"Thanks, man," he yelled from the retreating truck. "I'll get it back to you. I swear. In the mean time, mine's in the mess hall. You're welcome to it."

"No problem," came a voice just out of sight.

"Hey, it was good to get to know you."

"Likewise. Keep your head low."

"Low as I can go," was the reply as the truck drove away.

MB could see the shadow of the man standing near her as he watched the truck drive out of sight. She couldn't be sure but he seemed oddly familiar to her.

***

Then she was back on the lawn and reaching for the table to steady herself.

The young man spoke. "You know how sometimes the briefest of conversations can make the biggest difference?" the soldier was saying.

"Yes. I do." MB thought for a moment of the woman's shelter she donated to and how sometimes even the shortest of conversations can be uplifting to another human being.

The soldier continued, "That man eased my burden just a bit that day and I never got a chance to thank him."

"Is that it then?" she asked, sounding a bit put-out. "Is all this about an overdue thank you?"

"No, ma-am. I think that man can save my son's life."

She immediately felt bad about her attitude. "Okay," she softened. "What can I do?"

"All you need to do is give him that helmet."

"Really?" MB asked a bit incredulously. "And how am I supposed to do that?"

"The old woman said you'd know."

Made in the USA
Lexington, KY
03 June 2018